$16.95

n k

HEART IN THE CLOUDS

On a call-out, helicopter pilot Jillane Talbot finds that her passenger is none other than her estranged husband, the ruthless but devilishly handsome, Ash Carey. Jillane had run out on him five years earlier, and thought it best to regard their marriage as having ended. However, Ash has different ideas, and when he discovers an unbelievable secret that she has kept from him all these years, he vows to win her back.

JOY ST. CLAIR

HEART IN THE CLOUDS

Complete and Unabridged

LINFORD
Leicester

First published in Great Britain in 1994 by
Robert Hale Limited,
London

First Linford Edition
published July 1995
by arrangement with
Robert Hale Limited,
London

British Library CIP Data

St. Clair, Joy
    Heart in the clouds.—Large print ed.—
    Linford romance library
    I. Title II. Series
    823.914 [F]

    ISBN 0–7089–7740–5

Published by
F. A. Thorpe (Publishing) Ltd.
Anstey, Leicestershire

Set by Words & Graphics Ltd.
Anstey, Leicestershire
Printed and bound in Great Britain by
T. J. Press (Padstow) Ltd., Padstow, Cornwall

This book is printed on acid-free paper

To the fellas
Shane, Frank, John, Mick and Guy

1

JILLANE gazed down on the heather-clad hills where far below the shadow of the helicopter kept pace with her.

The radio crackled and a friendly voice demanded to know her whereabouts.

Jillane imparted the information, adding, "Felden Ridge is just ahead of me. I can see the landing pad."

"That's terrific!" came the enthusiastic reply. "Rightio then, bring it down!"

Jillane couldn't help smiling at the most unorthodox landing instructions she had ever been given.

"Thanks. Over and out."

It was a glorious day for flying. For the past fifteen minutes she had been travelling along the edge of the Northumberland national park and the vastness of the panorama quite took her breath away.

The climate hereabouts could be uncompromising. The temperate springs were all too short, the summers were invariably windswept, the winters bleak and snow-driven. But this was the start of autumn and the wild expanses were ablaze with colourful growth.

High on a hillside directly ahead was a sprawling bungalow nestling in a sheltered position between two peaks, its large picture windows reflecting the late afternoon sun. Her bird's eye view revealed extensive gardens and lush lawns. It was the only dwelling for miles around and access appeared to be by way of a ribbon of road winding up from the valley.

As she swooped in lower she distinguished several large flashy cars in a walled courtyard. Nearby two overalled men were working on a small helicopter similar to the one she was flying.

She wondered idly who could be the owner of such a splendid hideaway.

With a glance to check the dials on

the control panel, she took the cyclic in both hands and placed her feet on the yaw pedals. The subtle change in the rhythm of the rotor blades was comforting as the craft responded to her manoeuvres.

The landing pad appeared immediately below her, a large H marked in white concrete at the side of the lawn. To the other side stood a little group of people holding croquet mallets. They upturned their faces and shielded their eyes to watch her land.

She was almost down when she noticed a large glass-walled gazebo inside which two white-coated waiters stood beside a long buffet table. Another smile tugged at her lips.

She worked for Wyler's Wings, based in Denbridge, a few miles south-east of Gateshead, and was used to the routine ferrying of goods and passengers. Just occasionally she was called out on a mercy flight, to pick up someone stranded in the hills, or rush a sick person to hospital, but this was the first emergency when she had found a house party in full swing.

The helicopter skids touched down and the trees fringing the pad tossed wildly in the strong blast from the whirling blades. She saw the people on the lawn move back as their hair and clothes were whipped by the draught.

As soon as the rotors stopped turning a man, dressed in a safari shirt and shorts, hurried towards her. He was thin and wiry, with an untidy mop of fair hair and a freckled grin.

"Hi!" He waved. "You made pretty good time."

Recognising the teasing public-school voice of the person with whom she had been in contact over the radio, she unfastened her seat belt and climbed out.

She had stuffed her long hair into a black baseball cap to keep it from blowing across her face and as she removed it her mass of silky curls, the colour of ripening oats, slid about her shoulders. She sifted her fingers through it to coax it into some sort of order.

The man looked her up and down, noting every detail of her appearance — her tall trim figure, her delicate bone structured features, her eyes an unusual shade of periwinkle-blue. His mouth broadened into a grin and he grabbed her hand. "Hello! I'm Hugo Brooking."

"Jillane Talbot."

From their amusing exchanges over the radio, she had expected someone young and irresponsible. Well, he was certainly young, early twenties she supposed, but close to she detected a keenness in his eyes that belied his flippant approach.

"Do you play croquet?" He took her elbow. "Come and join the party."

"But . . . " She stared at him, puzzled. "Aren't you in a hurry to get to Sunderland? I thought it was an emergency dash . . . "

"No, no," he cut in. "There's plenty of time. And it's not me, it's the boss man. Meanwhile you must come and have some refreshment and a glass or two of wine."

"Well, if you're sure. But no wine, thank you. Not when I'm piloting."

"Ah yes."

"Besides." She looked down at her Levis and oversized Aran sweater. "As you can see, I'm dressed for warmth and ease of movement rather than partying. I really don't think I'm . . . "

"Oh come on! You look fine." He led her towards the buffet table inside the gazebo. "You're not from these parts, are you? Do I detect a slight East Anglian accent?"

"That's astute of you. I thought I'd lost my accent. I'm from Norfolk originally."

"You're a long way from home then."

"No, my home is in Denbridge now."

He beamed at her. "At the risk of sounding sexist, I must say it's unusual to find a woman piloting a helicopter.

I find it intriguing. How come?"

"There's nothing intriguing about it," she replied. "My dad used to fly planes and I was always interested in flying. He taught me as soon as I was old enough to sit in a pilot's seat and read the instruments. So flying a helicopter came easy."

"But you seem so young."

"I'm twenty-two." She laughed. "How old do you have to be?"

He shrugged. "You've got me there. It's something I haven't thought about."

One by one the dozen or so people who had been playing croquet abandoned their game and gathered round the little two-seater helicopter to stare in the windows at the controls before coming into the gazebo to stare at its pilot.

They were casually dressed but there was an air of affluence about them and Jillane would bet her last pound their clothes were designer-labelled.

Hugo introduced her to everyone present. There were a few impressive

7

titles among them — a doctor or two, a lady and a couple of sirs — but he reeled them off so fast that she forgot them immediately.

A waiter handed her a Royal Doulton plate and she browsed through a mouth-watering display of smoked salmon, pâté de foie gras, gateaux and exotic fruits. Again she refused a glass of wine but accepted a cup of coffee.

"Is this your house?" she asked Hugo.

"Heavens no! It belongs to the boss man. He's in his study, phoning and faxing various business contacts."

"And it's he I have to ferry to Sunderland?"

"That's right."

"Then shouldn't you tell him I'm here?"

"Best not to disturb him." He winked at the others. "He'll have seen the helicopter land so he'll come out when he's ready."

"Hm, best not to disturb him," repeated one of the women, grimacing to her companions. She turned to Jillane and said in a conspiratorial whisper, "He's not too pleased with Hugo at the moment. It was Hugo who crashed the boss man's own helicopter as he flew him in yesterday."

Hugo saw Jillane's look of concern. "It's all right, no-one was hurt," he forestalled her question. "It wasn't really my fault. It was foggy and I mistook the height from the landing pad, so we came down a bit hard and shot off into the bushes."

"Excuses, excuses!" came the chorus.

Hugo ignored the interruption. "There was only minor damage, but the machine will be out of action for a few days. You probably noticed the mechanics working on it as you flew over."

She nodded.

"The boss man has an important meeting in Sunderland and that's why you were sent for," Hugo explained.

The others drifted back to their game and Jillane took her plate and coffee cup to one of the little tables at the edge of the croquet lawn.

Even though they were several hundred feet above sea level, it was pleasantly warm, the peaks to either side of them forming excellent windbreaks. Before sitting down she pulled off her sweater and hung it on the back of the wrought-iron chair.

Hugo took the chair opposite and ran his eyes over her white T-shirt. "I have a weakness for beautiful blue-eyed blondes," he murmured.

There was a hoot of derisive laughter from the croquet players and somebody said, "And green-eyed redheads and brown-eyed brunettes. And all shades in between too, I shouldn't wonder."

Hugo was unabashed. "Take no notice of them. They're jealous. With good reason." He swelled with pride. "I'm boss man's personal assistant, on loan from Oxford University."

"Does he run his business from here?" asked Jillane politely between bites. "It must be difficult, having to keep flying in and out, at the mercy of the weather . . . "

"Boss man doesn't run the business from here," grinned Hugo. "He has offices in the Midlands and London and agencies all over the world. This is one of his weekend retreats." He looked thoughtful for a moment. "Though, come to think of it, he's never been really keen on weekends away. He'd much rather play tycoon than relax. If it weren't for me bullying him he'd never take a break." He leaned back in his chair and linked his fingers behind his head. "And while he's here it's as if his ear is welded to the phone."

Jillane gulped the hot coffee. "I used to know someone like him."

He seized on her rueful tone. "Oh-oh! Do I detect a thinly disguised broken heart? Want to tell Uncle Hugo all about him?"

"No way!" she replied emphatically, wishing she hadn't mentioned him. Till quite recently the experience had been too painful even to contemplate, let alone talk about. But everything comes to an end, she had discovered, and the day had dawned when she could speak his name without feeling bitter. It had been a relief to know she was free of his hold on her emotions and she had congratulated herself on her instinct for survival. However, the prospect of discussing her secrets with a perfect stranger did not appeal to her.

Hugo gave her a sympathetic nod and swiftly changed the subject. "I've told you about my boss. What's yours like?"

"Matthew Wyler? Oh, he's okay."

"Is he sweet on you?"

Jillane was unprepared for such a personal question and a faint tinge of heat warmed her cheeks. "No, he isn't," she lied.

"He must want his head examined." Hugo hit his forehead with his palm. "Oh lord! You might be engaged, or married even. There's bound to be someone, a beautiful girl like you. Unless it's the old story of little girl hurt, little girl not trusting again." He paused. "Is it?"

Her blush deepened. She couldn't make Hugo out. At first sight he seemed the usual stereotype lecher with all the clichéd approaches, but now she sensed there was more depth to him than she found comfortable. At least you knew where you stood with stereotypes.

She drained her coffee cup and rose from the chair. "Hadn't you better find . . ."

"No need." Hugo looked past her towards the bungalow. "Here he comes now."

A deep voice from behind her said, "I saw the helicopter land, Hugo. So where's the pilot?"

Jillane froze and for an agonising moment her features remained locked in a expression of disbelief. Oh God! It can't be! Please, please, don't let it be him! She stood transfixed, not daring to turn round lest her worst fears were realised.

13

Eventually she had to turn. As she did so, slowly, the colour went from her cheeks, jumbled thoughts paralysed her brain and she felt ready to faint.

Ash Carey stopped in his tracks, his face as white as her own. "Jillane! What the . . . !"

He had hardly changed, she thought, in the five years since she had last seen him. His eyes still glinted with that ruthless streak she had considered so profoundly disturbing. His expression was still as forceful and unrelenting as she recalled. He was perhaps even taller than she remembered and his mane of hair appeared blacker, thicker, more luxuriant. He wore a shell-suit which, though loose-fitting, could not disguise the aggressive vitality of his powerful body. She vaguely calculated he would be just the right side of thirty.

Hugo stepped between them. "I was going to introduce you," he murmured, "but you've obviously met before." He shrugged as they remained motionless. "Okay then, I'll introduce you anyway.

Jillane, this is Ash Carey, the boss man."

They stared through him. As if their obvious hostility were tangible, he ducked out of the way. "Ash, this is your pilot, Jillane Talbot."

"This is not Jillane Talbot," Ash grated out. "This is Jillane Carey. My wife!"

★ ★ ★

Jillane struggled inwardly to appear composed, but she suspected she failed miserably. Her thoughts had gone haywire, completely out of control, and her mouth had dropped open. Her legs felt as if they would collapse beneath her any moment and she was having difficulty breathing. As the truth seeped through to her brain that it really was him and not an hallucination on her part, it was as if she were gripped in the throes of some mysterious fever. How uncanny that the mere sight of him should throw her into such a spin, as if he still controlled her actions. Just a few minutes ago she had been congratulating herself on her recovery from the effects of Ash Carey, now she was plunged back into that black hole of despair.

She'd had dreams of this meeting, though nightmares might be a better description. She had fantasized about what she would say if they ever met again. Would she ignore him, be icily polite, or collapse in a heap at his feet? Now that the dream was reality she did none of those things. Instead she just remained there staring like an idiot while the minutes ticked by.

At Ash's announcement that she was his wife, a murmur of interest had rippled through the gathering of croquet players and all eyes were fixed on her.

"That's . . . not strictly true, Ash," she piped up at last, surprised by the high-pitched squeakiness of her voice. "We are . . . separated . . . "

"Unofficially!" he snarled. "For the

simple reason that you ran out on me!"

He seized her arm and the physical impact made her nerves contract, like a hedgehog rolling into a ball at at the first sign of danger. He'd always had the power to intimidate her and, as she mentally shrank from him, the preceding five years might never have been.

"Let me go!" she hissed, trying to break free.

He paid no mind to her plea. His fingers gripped like steel clamps. "We can't talk here. It's too public. Come indoors!"

Once again she tried to shake him off but he held on like a dog to a bone. "No!" she cried. "There's nothing to talk about. It's finished. Over."

He pushed her through the open french windows into what was plainly a study with a huge leather-topped desk, several filing cabinets and a well-stocked book shelf. "Finished it may be, Jillane, but there's plenty to talk about."

He released her at last and closed the doors firmly behind him. Rounding on her again, he said, "Whatever got into you? Going off like that without so much as a word of explanation? Have you any idea what you put me through with your thoughtlessness?"

"I tried to explain how I felt, over and over again," she said, pointedly rubbing her arm where his fingers had dug in. "You wouldn't listen to me, Ash. You never listened . . ."

He wasn't listening now.

"I searched everywhere for you. I was worried sick and out of my mind. Dammit, Jillane! You'd just given birth to a stillborn child. I couldn't begin to think what state of mind you were in. You'd disappeared from the face of the earth. For all I knew you could have been dead! Why didn't you have the decency to tell me to my face you were leaving me, or failing that, get someone else to tell me? Your stepmother for instance. But she was as baffled as I. At the very least you could have telephoned or sent a letter!" He moved towards her. "Tell me, where have you been all this time?"

For a moment she was overcome with guilt by his angry tirade. It was like old times, being shouted at and made to feel inadequate by him. But he had no authority over her now, she reminded herself. Not any more. She was older, more mature, no longer his child bride to be chivvied and made to consider herself a nuisance.

"Well, haven't you a tongue in your head?" he demanded. "Have you nothing to say to me?"

She straightened her shoulders and jutted her chin. "Be quiet!" she answered evenly, dredging up a modicum of self-esteem from the depths of her psyche. "Don't talk to me like that. That was always your trouble, bossing me about. I am not prepared to discuss the matter, now or at any time."

He stood before her breathing deeply

and she saw a nerve in his jaw begin to throb in the way she remembered. At the same time his hands clenched and unclenched and his body was rigid with suppressed fury, indicating he was holding on to his temper with extreme difficulty.

She observed at close quarters that he had changed after all. The lines on his cheeks and forehead were deeper and there were grooves beside his eyes. She also noted a silver hair or two in that thick mane. Only his eyes were the same, the unusual honey-brown colour she had liked to call butterscotch. Sometimes warm, sometimes brittle, in unguarded moments they could be a guide to his moods, but mostly his thoughts were hidden behind a mask of cool detachment.

She said quickly, "I came to ferry you to Sunderland and that is all I am going to do."

For timeless moments he stared at her, then suddenly he relaxed his angry stance. His eyes regarded her with interest now and she could almost see him noting the differences in *her* appearance.

At once she felt at a disadvantage in her serviceable working clothes. In the dreams she had always been impeccably gowned and coiffered when she came face to face with him again, not wearing jeans and T-shirt with her hair all over the place. Trust fate to intervene and show her in the worst light possible.

Her train of thought appalled her. What did it matter what she looked like or what he thought? He was nothing to her.

And yet it did matter. It mattered terribly.

"You look well," he murmured at last. His eyes toured her face, the tangled oaten hair, the periwinkle eyes wide with bewilderment, her lips trembling though she tried to keep them still. He added, "And quite, quite beautiful."

His compliment, delivered matter-of-factly, caught her off balance and her mouth went suddenly dry. "Thank you," she croaked. They were standing close together, almost touching, and she could smell the distinctive fragrance of his cologne. She recalled he had it made up specially for him by an aromatherapist in New York. She'd found a bottle of it among his belongings and he'd explained he'd used it since suffering a shoulder injury playing rugby at his public school when he was seventeen. It contained a subtle blend of pine and ginger with just a smidgeon of ylang ylang. As the half-remembered perfume invaded her senses the memories eddied about her, of being in his arms, tasting his kisses, feeling his skin against hers, and at once she was transported back to those five glorious days at the beginning of their turbulent relationship.

The unreality of the situation hit her and she swayed on her feet. She clutched the back of a chair for support and dimly heard him enquire if she were all right. Nodding she also conceded that those five days of love had been followed by two months of bitterness. After which she had run out on him.

She impatiently tossed the images away. At this moment it was imperative she kept her wits about her and did not go to pieces in front of him.

He had a bemused expression on his face. "This is too much of a coincidence to be true, your coming here to fly me to Sunderland." His eyes narrowed for a moment then gleamed in triumph. "Ah! I wonder . . . "

Going to the french windows again he opened them and hollered, "Hugo!" He turned back to Jillane. "I'll get to the bottom of this."

The fair-haired young man appeared, smiling all over his freckled face. "You called, boss man? Your wish is my command."

"You sound like the genie in the lamp," said Ash irritably. "And stop calling me boss man."

Hugo adopted an ingratiating expression and placed his hands palm to palm. "Anything you say, bo . . . er *Mister* Carey. Sir!"

Ash perched on the edge of the desk and crossed his long legs at the ankles. "This is your doing, isn't it, Hugo? Bringing Jillane here. Though how you managed to find her when I, using the best detectives in the country, failed . . . " He whistled softly. "You crashed my helicopter on purpose!"

"Ash!" Hugo's expression was pained. "You wound me to the quick."

"Shut up!" Ash pushed himself away from the desk and advanced menacingly towards the younger man. "What's it all about, eh? Why all this charade? Helicopter crashes and sending for Jillane! Why didn't you just tell me where she was?"

Hugo looked horrified and backed away in mock fright. "And have you go round to her place of work and cause a scene?"

"So you admit it?" muttered Ash. "You admit you are wilfully responsible for the damage to my helicopter? Can you think of any good reason why I shouldn't fire you on the spot?"

Hugo turned plaintively to Jillane. "That's all the thanks I get."

She had been standing there in a kind of trance listening to their conversation. The realisation that this confrontation had all been set up took its time filtering through to her overloaded brain and was still difficult to believe. But she gleaned a scrap of comfort from Hugo's reason for his actions. It would appear he knew where she worked, but not where she lived. She was thankful for that but wondered how long it would be before Ash discovered everything about her. Everything!

Hugo was addressing Ash again. "I can't take all the credit for finding her. In fact I can't take any. I had help." He glanced in Jillane's direction. "I was approached in the first place by someone who has her welfare at heart."

Jillane's mouth gaped again. "Who was it?"

Hugo smiled gently. "Think, my dear young lady, who loves you and is worried about you?"

Matthew Wyler! Jillane felt another wave of weakness breaking over her. Slowly she subsided into the chair behind the desk as the situation at last became clear. Matthew Wyler was fond of her. No, it went a lot deeper than that. He loved her. He wanted to marry her. But he knew there was no future for him as long as she remained married to Ash. So he had got in touch with Hugo and between them they had arranged for husband and wife to meet.

She trembled with indignation. How dared Matthew do this to her behind her back? How could he betray her to Ash while purporting to have her wellbeing at heart? She would have plenty to say to him when she got back to the office later this evening.

She was reminded of her mission and stood up. After several deep breaths she forced her panic to subside. What could Ash do to her, after all?

"If you really want to go to Sunderland, Ash," she said, "I'm leaving now." Outwardly calm, churning inside, she walked towards the french windows. "With you or without you."

"Very well." He glared after her. "I must see my secretary. I'll be just a moment."

He went out of the room and she heard his footsteps going along what sounded like a parquet-floored hall. A distant door opened and closed.

Hugo grinned sheepishly and ruffled his hair, Stan Laurel style. "Guess you're not too pleased with me, Jillane."

She gave a monumental sigh. "Huh! That's an understatement if ever I heard one!" A thought occurred to her. "Am I to ferry him back here again after his important meeting?"

"No, he's going straight to his home in Derbyshire, by train."

Well, at least that was something to be thankful for, she mused. But mention of his home in Derbyshire caused her a moment's sadness. She had been so unhappy there . . .

She went purposefully to the window and stared out at the croquet lawn. The game had finished and the players were relaxing in the gazebo, laughing and talking, glasses of wine in their hands. Beyond them the purple hills stretched away endlessly. It was really very beautiful and she let it calm her tattered nerves. "Who are all these people?" she asked for something to say. "What are they doing here?"

"Business acquaintances mostly," Hugo replied. "People to whom we owed hospitality. Their Rolls Royces and BMWs are parked behind that wall over there."

"Hm, I noticed them."

"They all offered to drive Ash to his destination but he wouldn't impose upon them. Besides it takes for ever to get down that winding hill and often the river at the bottom is in flood. He prefers flying in and out."

"So you called for a helicopter," she mused. "I do wish you hadn't. You don't know what damage you've done." With that she stepped out onto the grassy terrace and made her way down the steps and across the lawn to the chair where she had left her sweater.

Hugo trailed after her and watched her pull the garment over her head.

"Look, Jillane, I'm sorry I played an underhanded trick on you, but I'm not sorry I got you two together again." Thrusting his hands deep into his trouser pockets and gazing at the ground, he looked like a small boy confessing some misdemeanour to the headmaster. "I don't know what it was that made you hate each other — I'm a new boy around here — but I do know it's turned Ash into a heartless working machine . . ."

She gave a short laugh. "You're mistaken. He hasn't changed one bit. He was always a heartless working machine!"

He kicked at a tuft of grass. "You must have loved him once, for you to have married him . . . "

Two bright pink spots shaded her cheeks. "Please stop right there," she ordered. "You don't know the first thing about it. This is a private matter between Ash and me and it has nothing to do with you."

"It has plenty to do with me, actually," he answered passionately. "I don't like to see him drive himself this way. It's bad for him and bad for the corporation. Anything is better than him not knowing where you were. What if he wants to get married again? What if you do? Can't you see? Neither of you can make fresh commitments while you are tied together."

She was speechless.

He hadn't finished. "The sooner you two sit down round a table to sort something out, whether it's getting back together or separating officially, the better." He grinned, well pleased with himself. "So you see I acted in good faith. Things can only improve now."

She stared in disbelief. "You're wrong, Hugo, things can now only get worse!"

Ash came over the grass towards them. He had changed into a dark suit, a white shirt and silver tie. He looked handsome and worldly, the businessman that he was, and Jillane experienced an inexplicable little shiver running down her backbone.

In his wake was a woman, glamorous and statuesque, with flawless make-up and a great crown of auburn hair, burnished and vibrant and bound with a black ribbon. She was about the same age as he, give or take a year, and walked with the confidence of long association.

Jillane had always thought redheads could not wear pink successfully but the woman's clinging jersey jump-suit was stunning, outlining her curves and endless legs to perfection.

Sheridan! Still with him! Still pretending to be his secretary, no doubt!

"Hello, Jillane, it's good to see you again." Sheridan smiled and sounded as if she meant it.

Jillane swallowed a hard lump that threatened to choke her then, recovering her poise, murmured a greeting.

Sheridan handed Ash the briefcase she carried and stood on tiptoe to receive the brush of his lips against her cheek.

Sick at heart, Jillane turned away and walked over to the helicopter.

She climbed in and ran her eyes over the instrument panel, then she picked up the radio handset and made contact with air traffic control to ask if any change was likely in the weather and wind direction.

Ash had left Sheridan and Hugo and was saying goodbye to his guests who had swarmed out of the gazebo to see him depart.

At last he broke away from them and strode towards the helicopter with all the grace and power at the command of a successful man.

Once more a shiver assailed Jillane.

He watched her as he swung himself aboard, his gaze lingering unconsciously on her hair. She deliberately stuffed it back into the baseball cap.

He gave an almost imperceptible shrug and she immediately felt foolish. She was aware she would need more than a baseball cap to seal herself off from his devastating presence.

She wasn't looking forward to the flight to Sunderland with Ash Carey sitting beside her. As the crow flies it was a sixty mile trip and, cruising at a hundred and twenty miles an hour, should not take more than thirty minutes. Nevertheless, it promised to be the longest journey of her life.

2

THE co-pilot's seat doubled as a passenger seat. As Ash dropped into it and eased his long legs into the space in front, Jillane thought idly that the craft had not been built with him in mind. His presence dominated the cabin and she felt threatened again.

Catching sight of herself reflected in the side window she was surprised how calm and collected she looked. She only wished she felt it. It seemed a lifetime since she had landed on the heli-pad. Her mood had been carefree then, lulled by the beautiful scenery and the clement weather. She might have known she was heading for a traumatic experience. Life was like that, she thought. It set you up to knock you down again. Just when you decided it was safe to enjoy yourself along came something unpleasant to wipe the smile off your face.

This particular dilemma was all Matthew's fault. If only he'd spoken to her first instead of meddling in her affairs and creating this havoc.

Matthew! Having regarded him as a true friend she had entrusted her secrets to him, not realising he was capable of betraying her.

She could hardly credit his interference. He always seemed so caring and understanding. Even supposing he had considered he was acting for the best, it was still a gross invasion of her privacy — as well as being a crackpot idea. Why couldn't he mind his own business?

She chewed the inside of her cheek pensively. She hadn't been totally honest with Matthew, she had to admit. Maybe if she had told him the whole story he would have realised the deeper implications of his actions and the awkwardness of the position in which he had placed her.

She realised Ash was watching her, a look of impatience on his rugged face. "Shall we go then?"

"What?" She started nervously. "Oh yes, sorry."

She fastened her seat belt and looked to check he had done the same, relieved to see he had. Having to fasten it for him would have been too embarrassing. She wanted no further physical contact with him and leaned her knees as far as possible away from his.

This action brought an expression of grim amusement to his face and she wished she hadn't made her aversion to him so obvious. She wanted to appear detached, indifferent to his proximity, show him he had no control over her emotions, even though she had a suspicion it wasn't true. She was still in shock from meeting him and felt self-conscious about every move she made.

With her hand on the collective she switched on the rotor blades, reminding herself this was a job of work. She intended to behave as she would with any passenger. Polite and helpful, but distant.

She'd ferried all types, the nervous, the excitable, the blasé, and had had her share of amorous pests too. The gropers were the worst although she had found her thick clothing usually put them off. Women taxi drivers must have the same problems but they could at least stop the vehicle and get out. At fifteen hundred feet she couldn't. She was confident Ash did not pose any such trouble. No, his presence created a more subtle menace.

In a few moments they were airborne and banking to head in the direction of the east coast. As they levelled out without incident she felt Ash relax beside her. He must have been holding his breath and she smiled to herself. He'd always seen her as a child. Perhaps this would convince him at last that she'd grown up.

"Neat take-off," he remarked, his voice a low burr which sent her pulses galloping.

Jillane forced a smile. "Thanks." She realised she had also been holding her breath and expelled it slowly so as not to let him know.

"How long have you been flying helicopters?"

"Since . . . oh, a few years now. My father flew planes . . ."

"Yes, I remembered he'd been a flying man and had taught you to fly." Ash reached down to place his briefcase between his legs. "Because of that I checked every aircraft charter company in the country to try and find you. No wonder I drew a blank everywhere. The thought of you being a helicopter pilot simply didn't enter my mind."

He was speaking calmly, as if to a casual acquaintance, and she turned her head to regard him. The thrust of his jaw showed him to be anything but calm and she experienced a little pang of regret. It could have been so different . . . so wonderful . . .

He must have sensed her eyes upon

him. "Watch where you're going, Jillane," he said crisply. "We don't want any more mishaps. If I remember correctly, you are accident-prone."

She looked stonily ahead, inwardly seething. He referred, she knew, to her fall down the stairs five years ago. 'That old standby of the late late show,' he'd said at the time, making it clear he considered she had done it on purpose. 'Couldn't you think of something more original?'

So he was still bitter about what had happened and continued to blame her. Nothing had changed. After all this time she had returned to the status quo. Right down to Sheridan being in attendance.

From the beginning it had always been Sheridan. He would never admit it, but Jillane wasn't so gullible these days. Even then, back at the start, when she had been under the influence of his charisma, she hadn't believed his protests over Sheridan.

They were flying above a deep ravine

and Jillane cast her gaze unseeingly over the savage vista of crag and torrent. The light was beginning to fade from the sky and the autumn-tinted trees streaked the earth with long shadows, giving it a mysterious aura.

It was a simple run across the national park to Sunderland and she allowed herself to relax a little. Admittedly she had been anxious on take off because she was keen to appear professional and not give him any cause for complaint. It wasn't like her. She was a competent pilot, but she needed his approval apparently.

She guessed he had a score of questions to ask her which she was not prepared to answer. She forestalled him quickly with, "What's this meeting in Sunderland about?" Then, thinking it might be confidential, she added, "Sorry. I shouldn't have asked about it. Don't tell me if it's hush-hush."

"It's no secret," he replied, his eyes at once alive with suppressed fervour, his expression tense. "We plan to take over Barnard Tractors. The deal is in the last stages but there are still a few wrinkles to sort out. It's important I don't blow it."

"Barnard Tractors?" She was impressed. "But they're famous, practically a household name here in the north east."

"Exactly." He couldn't hide the triumph in his tone. "We wouldn't be interested otherwise."

Wheeling and dealing, she thought. Did he ever let up? She had not known him when he had taken over his father's company, J W Carey and Son, at the comparatively young age of twenty-one, but she had heard the story many times of how he had transformed the small straitlaced concern, supplying farm machinery to Derbyshire farmers, into one of the premier conglomerates in the world. Now it was called Carey International with branches in forty countries and a workforce of thousands. There couldn't be many people who were not familiar with its advertising slogan — 'Carey cares'. Why, a substantial part of the world's food was manufactured on Carey's machines.

He must be extremely rich and successful. She had lived with him in the family home, a rambling old mansion in Derbyshire, for the brief two months they were together, but she was aware at the time he also had an apartment near the company's London office.

She knew he had acquired a Greek island and other property in the intervening years — although she had not known about the bungalow back there in the hills. Despite her dislike for him she had kept up with his career, getting her information from the financial newspapers and the gossip columns. It seemed a contrary thing to do, but she could not help being fascinated by everything he did. She *had* loved him once.

He broke into her thoughts again. "Where have you been hiding yourself these past five years?"

"Oh, here and there."

If he thought she was going to give him her address he was mistaken. She could not afford to have him know her present circumstances. It would ruin everything she had built up for herself. If he found out he would trample on her dreams like so much sawdust.

"I see." A note of anger had crept into his tone. "Jillane, what got into you? Why did you run away from me? Weren't you happy?"

Happy? she thought. Had he been blind and so tied up not to notice how wretched she was?

"I'd rather not talk about it," she replied. "If you don't mind. It all happened a long time ago and raking over the past gets you nowhere."

He was quiet for a long while. She thought he might have dozed off when suddenly he said, "Do you want a divorce?"

She swallowed hard. It wasn't at all what she had expected him to say and she was caught off her guard. "A divorce?" She cast about for a plausible answer. "I really hadn't thought about it."

"Don't you want to marry that fellow?" His eyes bored into her. For an instant she thought she detected a hint of compassion in their cool honeyed depths but common sense told her it was a trick of the light. "The one who, according to Hugo, set you up today? The one who cares for you?"

She trembled violently. His words were reasonable but the delivery was sardonic. Ha! she thought. He's so sure of his fatal charm he doesn't think anyone could possibly match up to him.

No, that wasn't true, she admitted, her shoulders slumping. There was not an ounce of vanity in him. He must be aware of the exciting ambience surrounding him but he never traded on it.

He was waiting for her answer,

tapping his long fingers on the arm of his seat. "Well?"

"As I said, I hadn't thought about it. The matter never came up. I was married . . . am married . . . "

"I repeat, do you want a divorce?"

"Not particularly." God! That was the last thing she wanted. A divorce would mean contact with him, letters, phone calls, meetings. She had her own reasons for wishing to keep things as they were. Reasons she could never divulge to him.

"And what if I want a divorce?"

She swung round to stare open-mouthed at him. That was another thing that had not occurred to her. To learn that he had searched for her was rather flattering, but not if the reason were to obtain a divorce. The knowledge hurt. "So you can marry Sheridan?"

"My motives don't concern you."

She sensed a flush of heat creeping into her cheeks. He was right of course. It was she who had walked out. And yet, the mere thought of him marrying Sheridan sent unexpected tremors down her spine. She could not imagine what ailed her. She should be overjoyed. If he married Sheridan she would be free of him for ever.

"A divorce makes sense," he said evenly. "There's no point in carrying on with this pretence of a marriage. Whatever your plans are at the moment one day you might wish to remarry. I think a divorce would be best for us both. A clean break. I'll speak to my solicitor about it as soon as I return to Derbyshire. It should be quite a simple operation."

She felt a wave of dismay wash over her and almost let go of the cyclic.

At once he put his hand on her arm. "What's the matter, Jillane?" he asked harshly. "I thought a divorce was what you wanted. So what is the problem?"

His warm touch, seeping through her sweater to her skin, sent her nerves dancing erratically. As if mesmerised, she stared at his hand, at the pale blue veins and the smattering of fine hairs which made him appear human and vulnerable somehow. On his little finger was a signet ring with a jet stone embossed with a simple letter A in gold. Her gaze travelled to where the crisp white cuffs of his shirt had moved up to reveal a large multi-function chronograph, the kind aquatic sportsmen wore, and across her mind flitted a picture of him in a wet-suit. Did he still indulge in water sports or was he too busy 'playing tycoon', she wondered?

His maleness was stifling her and she grabbed a deep breath before thrusting his hand away. It was almost as if the old attraction lingered on between them, heavily disguised but relentlessly ticking away like an unexploded bomb.

How was she going to get out of this mess without the whole thing blowing up in her face?

"So that's it," she murmured, forcing her mind back to his question. "You told me you loved me, but you seem very eager to get rid of me . . . " She stopped. She was being ridiculous. It was as she would have reasoned five years ago. He would think her just the same, a silly kid who didn't know what she wanted. He might even think she wished to continue with the marriage because she loved him, which was laughable. But she couldn't tell him her real reason for needing to keep things unchanged and was aware she must keep her wits about her in case she let something slip which would give his astute brain a clue.

"It was you who left," he reminded her again.

"Yes."

"You didn't give our marriage much of a try," he accused her. "Two months, wasn't it? I had great hopes for us during those first five idyllic days in Scotland, but you certainly made a fool out of me. I didn't know what a spoilt brat you were."

★ ★ ★

She had been sixteen when they met, he twenty-three.

Till then she'd lived a sheltered life with her father and stepmother in Norwich. Not spoilt exactly, but cosseted and protected from the harsh realities of the world. Dad was to blame for that. She looked like her mother, who had died of pneumonia, and he was afraid of losing her too.

Jillane had every material thing she wanted but was a prisoner of her father's love. He kept a tight rein on her activities and vetted her friends. It was not surprising that the moment she had an opportunity to kick over the traces she did so with a vengeance.

Normally Keith Prichard would not dream of letting his precious only child go to Scotland for two weeks under canvas with nineteen other teenagers. But this was a girls-only orienteering course and she would be chaperoned, Miss Wooding assured him.

It was her stepmother who talked him round. Dorlene was only fifteen years older than Jillane and she recognised her need to get away from parental influence for a while.

Ash Carey was one of the instructors. Jillane didn't know it then but he was a businessman doing a week's stint as a break from his work. In his worn jeans and faded T-shirt, he appeared a romantic figure. She saw him as a beachcomber, a wanderer who went where the fancy led him. She fell in love with him there and then — as did the nineteen other girls — and was thrilled to discover she was one of the five girls in his team.

They were all over him as he taught them to snorkel and wind surf. But he was immune to their pathetic attempts at seduction and gave them no encouragement. He had probably been warned to behave, they reflected ruefully around the campfire.

On the Friday of the first week, the day before he was due to return to his business commitments, the girls were sent backpacking singly into the hills to see how well they could survive on their own. Jillane became hopelessly lost just as the weather took a turn for the worse with heavy rain and a hill mist closing in. Looking back afterwards she wondered if she had done it deliberately. First love, she acknowledged, could be a powerful force.

Darkness brought misery and fear until Ash arrived to rescue her. They'd had to spend the night in a survival hut wrapped in towels while their clothes dried by the fire. And that's when it had happened.

"Look out!"

She started as another helicopter loomed directly ahead of them. They were on a collision course and she froze.

Ash wrenched the cyclic away from her and pushed it over hard, falling across her as he did so. They missed the helicopter by inches.

His nearness was unnerving and she shied away from him like a frightened colt. It was galling to have him prevent an accident and she knew she should express her gratitude, but her throat had gone dry. In any case she could imagine his contemptuous reply. If only he would stop leaning on her and settle back into his seat!

He thrust the cyclic back to her and his eyes brimmed with scorn. "I'd prefer to get to Sunderland in one piece, if you don't mind," he intoned sarcastically.

"I'm . . . sorry."

He sank back into the seat. "So you should be."

He was doing it again, she thought, making her feel stupid and inadequate. It was her own fault. Instead of picking over old wounds she should be putting her mind to the matter in hand so as not to give him another chance to prove it.

But now she had started, she could not prevent those images of the past from crowding her mind.

That night in the rescue hut had

been a revelation to her. With the first stirrings of sexual awareness came the need for experience and, although both of them tried to resist the insane moment of no return, the inevitable happened and they were swept away on a rushing tide of desire.

Early the following morning the two of them slipped away to an Edinburgh hotel where Ash phoned his company to say he would be away another week. They spent five idyllic days there, so obviously in love, before he was called away to deal with some trouble at a new tractor factory in Senegal, on the west coast of Africa.

His secretary, Sheridan, had flown to Edinburgh with papers for him to study on the journey. He must leave at once, he explained. And Sheridan must accompany him.

Jillane refused to take him seriously. Beachcombers didn't have factories and secretaries. And one look at the glamorous redhead told her he was two-timing her.

He laughed and kissed her passionately. "Keep the bed warm, my darling! Remember I love you. I'll be back before you know it."

She begged him to stay but he insisted a great number of people depended on him. Were she older she would understand. And all the time Sheridan stood there smiling.

As he and the redhead drove off in a taxi to the airport Jillane decided she wouldn't be there when he returned.

The moment she was on the train heading south she knew she had made a mistake. She loved him. She should have waited. But, she reasoned, if he truly loved her he would find her — somehow.

He hadn't found her and she knew she had been fooling herself. If it had not been her it would have been one of the other nineteen girls.

Her father demanded an explanation as to where she had been. Miss Wooding had telephoned him about her disappearance and the Scottish police had been alerted. For the first time in her life she refused to answer any questions.

"I wish you'd concentrate on flying this thing!" Once more Ash interrupted her chain of thoughts. "What's the matter with you? Are you ill?" He arched his thick dark brows. "Perhaps you'd like me to take over the controls."

"No thanks. That won't be necessary."

He was right. She was behaving badly. She couldn't blame him for being annoyed. She took a few deep breaths and mentally chided herself. Why should she go to pieces just when she had begun to regulate her life and make plans for the future? Within moments of hoving into view again he was systematically demolishing every barrier she had erected against him. She shouldn't let him intimidate her like this. What happened to her when she was near him that set her on the same route to humiliation?

She supposed it all stemmed from

that first humiliation, when her father had driven to Ash's office to ask him what he intended doing about her condition.

Their passion that night in the hut had been spontaneous and Ash was horrified to realise the following morning that she had been unprotected. It was perfectly logical, virgins could not be expected to be on the pill. After that he made it his responsibility and they had put their faith in the old wives' tale about it being impossible to conceive the first time.

She was in her sixth month before she plucked up the courage to tell Keith she was pregnant. The scene was imprinted on her memory for all time, her father looking greyer and older than she had ever seen him, Dorlene, youthful-looking and glamorous, sitting on the arm of his chair trying to calm him down.

Jillane recalled the look of disbelief on his face as it dawned on him what she was trying to say. She had let him down in the worst possible way and later she thought she heard him weeping.

Her stepmother had been a wonderful ally. She advised an abortion, but Jillane's blood ran cold at the very thought of it.

Keith had forced her to tell him the name of the father. Then he calmly informed Miss Wooding he'd sue her for not chaperoning his daughter properly unless she gave him Ash's address.

"He'll marry you or I'll kill him," he declared.

"Please, Dad, I don't want him to marry me simply because of the baby . . . "

"There's no better reason. This is my grandchild!"

It was just after Christmas when Keith set off in a blinding snowstorm. He returned coughing and spluttering and plainly ill, but triumphant. "You marry him in two weeks' time."

It was only then she found out he was

the Ash Carey, of Carey International.

"I won't do it!" Jillane cried. "He doesn't really want to marry me."

"He does. He's prepared to care for you and the baby. You will do my grandchild a great disservice if you refuse him."

In due course Ash arrived at the house. But this was no beachcomber. This was a stranger in a business suit.

"Why didn't you come after me?" she asked accusingly. "You said you loved me."

"I wanted to, but Miss Wooding wouldn't give me your address. I threatened and tried bribery but she wouldn't budge."

"I don't believe you! Dad managed her all right."

"Well, I don't know how he did it." Ash looked irritable. "If we're throwing accusations about why didn't you wait for me?"

They glared at each other.

"Look, Jillane, I want to marry you. Isn't that enough?" He spoke slowly and clearly as if to a child. "We have our baby to think of now."

She could imagine her father's instructions. 'Tell my little girl you want her. Make it good or else.'

Everything depended on the wedding night, Jillane decided, but Ash did not come near her. He was frightened of harming the baby, he said, and they had separate bedrooms.

She felt in the way at *Grasslands*, Ash's mansion in Derbyshire. The builders were in knocking the rooms about and Ash was hardly ever there. He was still tied up with the new plant in Senegal. He seemed frantic with worry — because of her or the plant she didn't know, both probably — and wore a long face around the house. She couldn't help thinking it wasn't much to ask that he put his new wife before his stupid tractors. She was often tearful and conceded she must have been hard to live with.

Ash ordered her about a lot. He said it was for her own good, to get her moving — sitting about was bad for the baby — and lift her out of her depression.

Then there was Sheridan. She had an office in the old lodge-keeper's house and was always popping in and out pretending to be his secretary. And Jillane wasn't used to servants. And she was sick all the time . . .

She could have put up with all of this, but knowing Ash had only married her because of the baby was what hurt. He hadn't reiterated that he loved her and he clearly hadn't forgiven her for not waiting for him in Scotland.

Two tragedies occurred in quick succession and Ash was absent on both occasions. First, a month after the wedding, Jillane's father died from a heart attack. She was desolate and guilt-ridden remembering how he had gone out in the snow because of her. She badly needed someone to talk to.

The moment he heard Ash flew home from Senegal to comfort her and promised to stay in order to be present at the birth of their child.

It was a promise he couldn't keep and presently he and Sheridan were summoned to Senegal yet again.

"Don't worry, I can sort it out in a couple of days," he told Jillane. "There's plenty of time."

"No-one is indispensable," she reasoned, dragging her swollen body upstairs after him.

"You're too young to understand," was his stock answer.

She watched him go from drawer to drawer in his bedroom. "I don't know why you bother to unpack that bag."

"Poor thing. You'll feel better after the baby's born. We'll go away afterwards for a holiday." He was racking his brains for something to sweeten her. "Why don't I ring Dorlene and invite her to stay for a few days to keep you company? I expect she's lonely without Keith."

"If you like," she replied disconsolately.

But she brightened when her step-mother's Volvo Estate drew up outside the house. Dorlene greeted her warmly, only too pleased to be needed.

The following day the two of them visited an exhibition of lace-making in Newark-on-Trent, twenty miles away. As they passed a row of telephones in the foyer Dorlene suggested Jillane put a call through to Senegal.

Ash was 'extremely busy', Sheridan said, but she fetched him. He sounded as if he was having an unusually bad day.

"Really, Jillane. Can't you leave me to get on with things and not keep bothering me? The sooner I finish things here the sooner I'll be home. Goodness, you're not a child . . . "

Jillane banged the receiver down. Feverish suddenly, her one thought was to get out into the fresh air. It was then, blinded by tears, she stumbled and fell headlong down the stairs leading to the exit.

There was no time to drive to the Chesterfield nursing home where a room had been booked for her so

Dorlene rushed her to the nearest hospital.

The young doctor looked grave as he examined her. Taking Dorlene aside, he said, "I'm afraid your stepdaughter is going to lose her baby."

If only Ash had been there when Jillane had needed him. It seemed like the final betrayal.

3

ARRANGEMENTS had already been made for Jillane to land the helicopter on the roof of a floodlit building in the heart of Sunderland and she was keeping an eye open for the place. She had landed there before so it presented no problems but she was pleased when it appeared below them. Flying in the dark was always tricky and she could not afford to lose any more concentration.

She executed a perfect landing, the skids coming down exactly on the white markings.

Ash seemed surprised. "Well done!" He glanced at his chronograph. "You've made good time. Thanks."

"I can get some things right."

He grabbed his briefcase from between his feet. "I've no doubt you can." The butterscotch eyes were mildly derisive.

"You've still got that chip on your shoulder though. But you're in the right job. Your heart always was in the clouds."

"What chip?"

"The one labelled 'do it my way'." He watched her steadily. "Haven't you learned anything these last five years? The world doesn't owe you a thing, Jillane. It's all compromise. You get out what you put in. Come down to earth!"

She wriggled uncomfortably under his scrutiny. There was only one way to deal with this kind of accusation, bite back! "Well, really! Coming from you, that's priceless." She gave a mirthless laugh. "When I want a lecture, I'll let you know."

"Will you, Jillane? Will you really?" The lowering of his voice to a sensually evocative pitch did strange things to her heartbeat. For a moment she ransacked her mind for a clever reply but only managed to come up with, "Oh, shut up!"

He had been about to rise but remained in his seat and regarded her stony expression. "You know? When we first met I thought you had a sunny disposition. I loved your laughter when we were together in Scotland." He placed his hand over hers once more. "What happened to you?"

His touch sent a shivery sensation oscillating through her. She didn't want to be reminded any more of Scotland. It was too painful. Best to answer tritely. Otherwise she might burst into tears. "That's a very good question. You happened to me, Ash Carey, that's what!"

She expected an angry come-back but he did not rise to the bait. Instead he said smoothly, "You're trembling, Jillane."

"I am not!" She snatched her hand away as if from a burning flame. "Unless it's with indignation."

He rose to his feet, stooping so as not to hit his head against the roof. He appeared self-contained and confident and she only hoped he didn't suspect the upheaval that was taking place inside her, rendering her nerves raw. So much for her belief that she had put the past behind her.

She got up and opened the door for him then swiftly bent back out of touching distance in that confined space. The manoeuvre was not lost on him and his lips slanted momentarily.

She waited for him to alight but he remained where he was. Suddenly without warning his hand shot out and his lean fingers curled round her chin.

She quaked with alarm. Was he going to kiss her? She prayed not.

He studied her features as if memorising every detail, from the hostile eyes to the trembling lips.

"Don't . . . "

"Don't what?" he enquired silkily.

"Don't . . . " She couldn't say the word and gave a little choke.

"Kiss you?" he finished for her. "Why not? For old time's sake?"

She looked briefly at his mouth,

curving slightly, lips parted, and a great shuddering breath escaped her. "I'd . . . rather you didn't."

"Don't worry, I wasn't going to." There was a wry edge to his tone, almost of self-mockery. "Far be it from me to force you to do something you might regret."

He released her and they stared at each other for what seemed an interminable time.

Finally his eyes travelled upwards and he burst out in exasperation, "I wish you'd get rid of that stupid hat!"

She raised her hand to stop him removing it but he was too quick for her. The cap landed on the floor and her hair flowed over her shoulders in a glossy shower.

"That's better," he murmured, his appreciative gaze raking her tresses.

She scraped them back and desperately put her mind to her work. To get the situation back on the rails, she said formally, "Thank you for travelling with Wyler's Wings." To her chagrin, her voice grew croaky. "I hope you'll travel with us again."

"Oh, I will." His laugh was feather-soft as he moved towards the door.

She watched him climb down, ducking instinctively under the spinning rotors.

He cupped a hand to his mouth. "We'll have to get together sometime to sort out what we're going to do," he shouted, his eyes gleaming through the darkness like points of fire.

She paused in pulling the door into place. "What do you mean? Sort what out?"

"Us. Our so-called marriage."

The draught from the blades tousled his hair, giving him that beachcomber look again and she swallowed hard. Darn him! Why did he have to turn up in her life now just when she was beginning to feel confident again?

"Don't bother, I'm all right as I am," she replied but her words were whipped away by a sudden gust of wind.

He touched his temple in a salute then turned and strode towards a door.

A moment later he had disappeared from her sight.

Jillane dropped back into her seat and sighed, her fingers idly stroking the cyclic. She felt weak and dizzy as if she'd been kept short of oxygen. Ash had that effect on her. His reappearance in her life put her in a quandary. She was at a loss to know what to do for the best, to stay put and face the consequences of this day's mischief or to make another run for it. It wouldn't be so easy this time. One thing was certain, now that he had found her he would go on digging. He wouldn't let her escape until he knew all about her current situation. He was nothing if not thorough.

She closed her eyes and allowed the relentless memories to eddy about her.

She had played a dirty trick walking out on him but there had been no other course of action she could have taken.

She remembered so well their last meeting.

Dorlene had put another call through to Senegal and demanded to speak to Ash to tell him the heartbreaking news.

He had wanted to return at once, but Senegal airport was affected by a strike of customs men. The only way he could get out was by travelling overland to The Gambia and catching a plane from there. It took three days by which time Jillane had discharged herself from hospital and returned to *Grasslands*.

Ash arrived tired and dishevelled. He was in a terrible state mentally and filled with remorse, blaming himself for everything that had happened.

Her ordeal in hospital had debilitated Jillane. She was unable to relate to him and he had mistaken her reticence for indifference. He had accused her of not wanting the baby in the first place, of feeling trapped into marriage by it, all the things she silently applied to him.

She did not attempt to deny any of it. What did it matter now?

So they heaped bitter accusations on

71

each other and the next day, after he had departed for the office, she phoned for a taxi to take her to the railway station. She had no idea where she was going, she only knew that to save her sanity she had to put as much distance between her and Ash as possible.

Five years ago and yet it was as clear in her mind as if it had been last week.

★ ★ ★

Fate certainly knew how to mess up tidy lives, Jillane reflected as she flew the helicopter back to Denbridge. She had thought she was over Ash and suddenly she wasn't so sure. Oh, she knew she didn't love him any more, that was obvious, but it was quite plain he still held some attraction for her. Perhaps he always would. She *had* loved him once.

But she would be a fool to let him interfere in her new life. She'd been through hell and lived to tell the tale.

She was happy and contented. Life was even, predictable. And that suited her fine.

Just before nine she touched down on the private airstrip belonging to Wyler's Wings. It was part of a larger commercial airport and the far side of it thronged with people catching the night flights.

She crossed the tarmac, picking up wolf whistles from a couple of mechanics working overtime on a Piper Cherokee. Any other time she would have rewarded them with a friendly grin but she wasn't in the mood for grinning and marched past, head held high.

She reached the long low building with 'Wyler's Wings' painted over the door. Most of the place was in darkness but she saw a tiny strip of light glimmering from a side window and guessed Matthew was still at his desk. He was bound to be. He never went home while one of the pilots was still flying.

She felt her way through the little reception room and opened the office door.

An angled lamp stood on the desk shedding its bright beam over Matthew's brown hair as he sat poring over a weather chart.

He looked up and his serious grey eyes lit with pleasure. "Jillane, at last!" He stood up and she saw he wore a light blue flying-suit with the logo of the company — a winged chariot — on the pocket. "I've been worried about you."

She knew that wasn't true. He would have contacted her by radio if it had been the case, but she understood what he meant. "With good reason," she said, placing the log book and keys on the desk. "Did you have to tell Ash Carey all my business?"

"Oh-oh!"

It was a day for reminiscing. Travelling away from Ash that day she had changed trains a couple of times and ended up in Denbridge, a small market town a dozen miles inland from the north-east coast. After making enquiries she had learned there was a helicopter charter firm just outside the town reported to be looking for a replacement pilot.

She had told Matthew her surname was Talbot — it was the make of a car standing outside the window — and that she'd lost her employment papers, her P45 and so on. She could sense he didn't believe her but he gave her the job all the same. Although she knew nothing about helicopters, she was proficient at flying a plane and expressed her willingness to learn. He taught her personally and within six months she was a fully-fledged helicopter pilot.

She evaded Matthew's outstretched arms and flopped into a low armchair. "It's not every day I'm asked to fly my own husband to Sunderland."

Matthew groaned and for a moment looked shamefaced. "You don't seem too pleased with my intervention!"

It was almost word for word what Hugo had said.

She bent to remove her boots. "I wish you hadn't interfered in my personal affairs. I am very annoyed with you."

"Jillane!" He sounded hurt. "You know how I feel about you and why I did what I did."

She knew. He loved her and wanted her to get a divorce so that they could marry. But she wasn't going to be rushed into another marriage. The existing one was causing enough headaches. Besides she had no desire to contact Ash again and there was no way of obtaining a divorce without doing so.

It wasn't really Matthew's fault. It was hers for confiding in him. He was a sympathetic character, like Hugo, and she was apt to drop her guard when with him. In a weak moment she had told him her troubles and look what had happened! You just could not trust anyone with a secret.

"The way you feel about me is no

excuse," she rejoined, meaning to let him know how she felt before burying the incident. "I told you things I didn't wish repeated and you went behind my back and contacted Ash's personal assistant. How could you!"

"I'm sorry, my dear." He scratched his head. "I really thought I was acting for the best."

He looked wretched and she relented a little. "Yes . . . well. I'd be obliged if you don't give him my address . . . " She heard Matthew's sharp intake of breath and jumped to her feet. "Oh no! You didn't give it to Hugo!"

He came round the desk and gently caught her shoulders. "Calm down, Jillane. You had to meet the man some time . . . "

"Did I?" she interrupted, staring up at him wide-eyed. "Who said so? I was doing very well keeping out of his way till you barged in telling all my secrets. I've never felt so foolish . . . "

"You had to meet him some time," Matthew repeated evenly, "to clear up this mess in both your lives. You don't love him. So why stay married to him? It's best to get it all settled."

Her eyes glittered. "Best for whom?"

"For you. For me." He drew her towards him. "For him too, most likely."

He tried to kiss her but she ducked out of his arms.

"Jillane . . . forgive me."

"I shall have to think about that."

He thrust his hands in his pockets and hunched his shoulders. "Was it traumatic, meeting him again?"

"I'd rather not talk about it." She picked up the boots and padded in her socks to the door. "I've had enough discussion for tonight. I'm going home. I'm tired and I want to think."

He bounded after her and managed to drop a peck on her cheek before she escaped. "All right," he called after her. "I'll see you tomorrow."

He was all right really, she conceded, gentle and sincere. Not like some people! He'd been jilted once, a long time ago, and was inclined to distrust women. At thirty-one he had considered himself a confirmed bachelor — then she had come on the scene.

She located her red Ford Escort in the brightly-lit car park and put on a pair of flat driving shoes which she took from the boot.

It took fifteen minutes to drive through the town and out the other side, to a quiet suburb where *Rose Villa*, the terraced house she had rented for the past five years, was situated. The Victorian dwelling, with its dust-harbouring nooks and crannies and big old marble fireplaces had been rather dilapidated then, but cheap and all she could afford. With tender loving care she had turned it into a comfortable home so that now when she could have afforded better she was content to stay where she was.

She let herself into a little hall crowded with coats on pegs and flowering plants and pushed open the door to the sitting-room.

Vikki Jones was dozing on the couch before a flickering television set and she jumped as Jillane gave her shoulder a gentle prod.

"There you are, Mrs Talbot." The pretty teenager, her hair cropped like a boy's, yawned and stretched and glanced at her watch. "Crikey! Is that the time? You're later than usual."

"Yes, I'm afraid I was ferrying a tricky customer to Sunderland." Jillane went to the phone. "I'll just get a taxi for you." She dialled and waited, covering the receiver with her hand. "I really am sorry. The trouble is I never know for sure how long I'll be."

"Oh, don't be sorry." Vikki grinned. "It doesn't matter to me." She went out to the hall and returned with her duffel coat as Jillane replaced the receiver. "You look all in, Mrs Talbot. You'll be wanting to get to bed." Another yawn. "And I shan't mind getting to mine."

"Yes, I am tired," Jillane admitted,

opening her purse. "It's been a very trying day. How much do I owe you?"

The girl did a mental calculation, staring at the ceiling, and named her fee. "I feel a fraud accepting money for a job that is so pleasant." She took the notes Jillane passed over. "I wish all my jobs were as nice."

"I really appreciate everything you do," said Jillane, turning off the television set. "I'd better warn you though, I might be going away for a short time, so I don't know when I shall need you again."

"Oh, I am sorry about that." Vikki shrugged on her coat. "Nothing serious, is it?"

"I'm not sure but I'll be in touch."

The hoot of the taxi horn cut across her words and they said their goodnights. Jillane waited till the taxi had driven away before closing the door and running up the steep narrow stairs.

A night-light burned in the little rear bedroom and she tiptoed in to gaze down at her five-year-old daughter sleeping peacefully, her thumb in her mouth, a teddy-bear clutched in her arms.

Jillane listened to the child's steady breathing. "Oh, Pepper," she whispered, gently smoothing the dark locks from the soft forehead, "it looks as if we're going to have to steal away again."

There was no hiding the fact that this was Ash's child. Apart from the identical colouring and texture of their hair, they walked the same, talked the same, had the same firm thrust of the chin, the same butterscotch eyes. Pepper had also inherited some of Ash's traits, like his determination and single-mindedness. All the time Jillane was able to gaze on Pepper she was not likely to forget what the child's father looked like.

She sat on the end of the bed wondering what to do. Ash must never know of his daughter's existence even if it meant their packing up and moving on. Jillane had gone to great pains to hide Pepper from him and now, through no fault of her own, all her efforts were in jeopardy.

She had known her marriage was a mistake from the very first day. Ash didn't want a wife, especially one as gauche and vulnerable as she. It had pleased her to think she was escaping from her father's prison, but she soon realised she had only changed one set of bars for another.

As she had lain in the hospital bed, in excruciating pain and haemorrhaging badly, she was convinced she would lose the baby. And the worried expressions of Dorlene and the doctor confirmed her worst fears.

Perhaps it was for the best, she consoled herself. Ash didn't want the baby. What sort of life would it have had with an unloving father?

There was a strong possibility she herself would die also. She almost hoped she would.

As they waited through that long night, it was Dorlene who planted the tiny seed of deception in her brain.

"Well, at least you won't have to stay with Ash now if you don't want to. You married for the baby's sake. No baby, no reason."

That was true, thought Jillane, and she resolved that if she lived she would get out of his way. It was only fair. She would be doing him a favour. He had no need for a wife and family. How much easier his life would be if she were no longer in it.

However, the next morning Jillane, against all the odds, was safely delivered of a healthy baby girl.

Dorlene was overjoyed as she held her step-granddaughter for the first time. "So it's back to Ash after all." She raised expressive eyebrows. "Or is it? Does he have to know?"

"Of course he does!"

But as the day wore on she found the idea of leaving Ash spinning round in her subconscious. He thought the baby was dead and was probably relieved. He needn't know it had lived, needn't ever have to feel guilty about neglecting it. The more she sifted through the possibilities the more she told herself it would solve everything.

On leaving the hospital Jillane placed the baby in Dorlene's care then returned to *Grasslands* to see Ash and explain about the stillbirth.

When he arrived and she saw the state he was in she almost broke down and confessed the truth.

"It's all my fault," he kept saying. "I forgot how young you are. I never should have left you."

He seemed genuinely dismayed about the loss of the baby and she was torn between his peace of mind and freedom for them both.

She reasoned it was perfectly natural for him to be upset but that time would quickly heal. Wouldn't it?

Then they'd had that disagreement about the fall and he had stormed off only to return thirty minutes later full of apologies and begging her forgiveness.

"I'll make it up to you, my darling,"

he assured her. "I'll spend more time with you and as soon as you're well we'll try for another baby."

She had decided she must tell him the truth but at that moment Sheridan phoned to say he was needed urgently back in Senegal.

He was thrown into a whirl of indecision and Jillane watched him wrestling with his conscience. "Just this once," he said. "Then I'll delegate. I promise."

That was enough for Jillane. After all she'd been through he was still putting the job before her. She was tired of his promises and knew he would never change.

Dry-eyed she watched him drive off then she packed her things and travelled to Norwich to collect Pepper from Dorlene. She would have liked to stay with her stepmother in her old home but knew Ash could trace her there. She swore Dorlene to secrecy and set off for the station.

It hadn't been easy bringing up

a child alone but plenty of mothers were forced to cope with the problem these days. To start with she hadn't an inkling of how to look after a baby. But she learned. And, having a well-paid job, she was better off than most. Because Matthew was fond of her, she was allowed to choose the flying jobs she accepted, leaving her time to enjoy her daughter's growing up and not have to rely too much on babysitters and minders.

As Pepper grew so did Jillane, mentally and spiritually. No longer the naive selfish child Ash had married but someone who could stand on her own two feet and look the world in the eye. Many times she felt guilty and mentally regretted the wrong she had done. If only she could turn the clock back to that fateful day she would have acted so differently. But the deed was done.

Once or twice she had reached for pen and paper to write to tell him of Pepper's existence. Then she would see photographs in the press of him pulling off some big deal or flying to foreign parts, always with the lovely Sheridan by his side, and she was lulled into believing she had done the right thing after all. Until today.

4

"EAT up, Pepper. Don't play with your breakfast." Jillane turned back to the sink and squirted washing-up liquid into a bowl of hot water. "We're going out."

The dark-haired child, dressed in a scarlet track-suit, stirred the cornflakes and gazed solemnly at her mother. "Where are we going?"

Jillane held a tumbler up to the light. "I thought we'd visit Uncle Matthew at his home, as it's Saturday." At least it would get them out of the house. "You like him, don't you?"

"He's all right." Pepper shovelled the remainder of the cornflakes into her mouth and got down from the table. She was going to be tall, like her father, thought Jillane.

She was on edge worrying that Ash might have discovered where she lived.

It only needed for him to catch a glimpse of Pepper and he would know without a shadow of a doubt she was his daughter. Then all hell was bound to break loose.

She should never have attempted to deceive him, but she had and there was no changing that fact. It had been her decision and she had no choice but to follow through.

She had covered her tracks so well. She had a new name and a new address, a new identity almost. Now just as she had begun to relax and think she was free Matthew had interfered and she had started feeling nervous again.

She was sure Hugo Brooking didn't know of the existence of Pepper, otherwise he would surely have mentioned her to Ash. And Ash would have raged and demanded to know where his daughter was hidden.

Matthew, wearing old denims, was working in his garden when they arrived at the converted farmhouse.

"Why, this is a nice surprise," he greeted them.

Pepper went off to look at his rabbits and he invited Jillane indoors for coffee. She had changed into a simple white shirtwaister, tightly belted to emphasize her neat waist. His eyes, used to seeing her in her bulky flying clothes, blatantly appraised her.

"You look lovely with the light from the window behind you shining on your golden hair," he said huskily. "You're giving me a foretaste of how it could be if we were to marry."

His words caused her a moment's uneasiness. She wasn't ready to jump into marriage again so soon. Perhaps she never would be ready. But she didn't want to hurt him by saying so. He was a kind man and he had been good to her. She wished she could feel more emotion for him, as he deserved, but she couldn't, so she said nothing. Her attitude caused her more pangs of guilt because she was taking from him with no intention of giving in return. She hoped time might remedy the situation.

"I hope you've forgiven me for interfering," he went on. "I'd hate to do anything to upset you."

"I've forgiven you," she grinned. "I can't stay mad at you. I only hope Ash doesn't find out where I live. If he sees Pepper . . . "

Matthew drew in his breath sharply. "You mean he doesn't know about her?" He scratched his head. "Jillane, am I hearing you right?"

She had the grace to look guilty. "It's a long story."

"I've got plenty of time."

Haltingly, without too many details, she told him what had happened. "So you see why I was angry with you."

"Yes." He whistled softly. "I really put my foot in it. You should have told me, you know."

★ ★ ★

When a week had passed and Ash had not materialised, Jillane began to relax. Perhaps she was being paranoic thinking he was all-seeing and all-conquering. Perhaps he was just a man after all.

No, she didn't think that. And the following Saturday he proved her right.

She had put on her old clothes and piled her hair on top of her head ready for housework. As she stood on the upstairs landing putting clean sheets away in the linen cupboard, she heard a powerful car drive along the road and stop outside.

She saw from the window a white Lotus Esprit and there was no mistaking the dark head of the man who alighted. For a moment her limbs felt paralysed.

He gazed up at the house, checking all the windows, and she drew back hastily, thankful for the thick net curtains. Horrified, she watched him start walking towards the front door.

The sound of the doorbell echoing through the house brought Jillane to life. She ran into the bathroom and looked frantically out of the rear window. Pepper was playing on a make-shift swing Matthew had rigged up for her at the end of the garden behind a thick cluster of hazel trees. There was no rear entrance so she was safely hidden for the moment.

"Stay there, my darling." Jillane willed the silent message to her daughter. With her heart beating like a pile-driver working overtime, she perched on the edge of the bath as the bell rang again.

There followed a lengthy silence after which she heard the footsteps going back along the path and there came the sound of the car door opening, then more footsteps. What *was* he doing?

At last came the shutting of the door, the springing to life of the powerful engine, the roaring away of the car.

As the silence returned, Jillane realised she was shaking like an aspen leaf. A glance in the mirror above the wash basin showed her face a deathly white. She waited an agonising ten minutes then forced herself to go down the stairs. As if he were still there, she scuttled past the front door and hurried to the kitchen where she filled the kettle and put it on the stove to make a much-needed cup of tea.

She dropped a tea bag into the pot and leaned against the table as her heart-rate returned to normal. It was then, looking along the hall towards the front door that something bright caught her eye. Through the frosted glass she could see something, a big blob coloured red and yellow, lying on the floor of the porch. Curiosity led her to go to the door and press her nose to the glass. She could just make out a large bunch of roses!

She unlocked the door, opening it a few inches to take a better look.

"Good afternoon, Jillane."

Her heart seemed to do a double somersault. Her palms grew moist. An ache spread over her limbs. She wondered vaguely if this was what a heart attack felt like.

Ash wore a short leather jacket with light-coloured trousers and he was leaning nonchalantly against the trellis, his hands thrust into his pockets, his feet crossed at the ankles. The light breeze ruffling his hair gave him a carefree, almost rakish appearance.

She leapt swiftly to close the door but he moved like lightning. She couldn't believe her eyes. One moment he was beyond the door, the next he was standing beside her in the hall. On the way he had somehow managed to scoop up the roses.

She gasped. "How . . . ?"

"Quite simple," he interrupted, pushing the door to behind him. "I parked the car along the road and walked back."

"I meant how did you know where . . . "

Once again she wasn't allowed to finish her sentence. "I trailed Matthew Wyler to this house the other evening.

An enquiry at the local newsagents told me what I wanted to know."

"Go away!" she hissed as fear welled up inside her. "This is my home. You have no right to come barging in here . . ."

"I have every right to call on . . ." He paused dramatically, "my wife!"

In the kitchen the kettle was steaming. He hurried into the room and placed the roses on the table then turned the gas down low. After that he calmly added another tea bag to the pot she had prepared and poured the boiling water in.

She dashed after him, surreptitiously kicking Pepper's little wellingtons under the cabinet. "What do you think you're doing?"

He gazed on her kindly and an unexpected smile darted to his lips. "You look like you could do with a cuppa."

She recovered her wits. "Get out of here!"

He calmly walked to the cabinet,

took down two mugs and placed them on the table.

She viewed him with hostile eyes. He had always seemed larger than life to her, having the kind of presence that could never be ignored. He was taller than anyone she knew and the leather jacket gave him a slightly menacing air. Contrarily he was also pleasing to look at. He had the gaunt cheeks and long black lashes of a poet balancing the firm jaw and calculating gaze of a man of action. It was a fascinating combination which was bound to intrigue most people, she conceded, especially women.

She swallowed a hard lump which had lodged in her throat and began again. "I'm busy. I've invited . . . someone to dinner and I shall soon have to get a salad ready."

He seized on her hesitation. "Matthew Wyler, I suppose." The butterscotch eyes, so benign a moment earlier, hardened to angry pebbles. "A very cosy arrangement!"

"What do you mean?" She suddenly caught the drift of his insinuation and her cheeks flared. "Now just you look here . . . "

"No, just you look here, Jillane." He calmly poured out the tea. "Matthew seems to spend a lot of time here. The inference is obvious. I'm not blind."

"He calls round sometimes," she replied coldly. "But it's not what you think."

He added the milk and his eyebrows raised derisively. "Really? What's wrong with him?"

He put sugar in one mug and offered her the other. "There you are, just as you like it."

"I've changed my habits," she snapped. "I like sugar in my tea now," she lied. "Lots of it!"

"I beg your pardon." He put in four spoonsful and stirred it thoroughly then tapped the spoon noisily against the mug. "There you are then."

She took it and he watched fascinated as she raised it to her lips.

It tasted horrible. "Lovely," she said, placing the mug on the table and thinking what a trivial victory she had scored.

His laugh irritated her intensely.

She strove for normality. "What are you doing here?" she asked. "Shouldn't you be out buying a bankrupt company or two?"

"I came to find out what you wanted to do about our marriage." He perched against the table, nursing the mug in his hands. "We can't go on like this, that's for sure. We are neither married nor divorced but in limbo." He looked around again, pointedly taking in an old jacket Matthew had inadvertently left hanging behind the door after he had helped her with the gardening. "Doesn't he want you to get a divorce and marry him?"

"We haven't discussed the matter." She traced the pattern on the Formica table-top with the tip of her finger. "What about you? Is there anyone waiting for you to divorce me? Apart from Sheridan?"

He frowned so deeply his eyebrows met. "You're not still accusing me of having an affair with my secretary, are you?" He ran one hand in an impatient fashion through his dark locks. "Sheridan has never interested me in the romantic sense, nor I her."

"Why are you still bothering to lie to me?" she asked scornfully. "You can admit you love her now, so why not do so?"

"Because I don't."

"Oh, there's no talking to you." Jillane's ears were primed for sounds of Pepper coming down the path. Her daughter loved playing on the swing but had been engaged in that activity for most of the afternoon. Any moment she was going to tire of it and come indoors to ask what was on the television.

Jillane poured the contents of her mug into the sink and ran the tap for a moment to rinse it before placing it upside down on the draining board. Briskly she said, "Well, I've got to see about the dinner. And you must be busy. I think you'd better leave."

He drained his tea. "Not till we've talked, calmly and without malice, about what we are going to do."

"I'm not going to do anything." She brushed past him and started taking various vegetable cutters from the dresser cupboard. "You decide what you want to do and let me know."

He turned to the sink, rinsed his mug and inverted it next to hers on the draining board. He really looked as if he might leave and she held her breath in anticipation.

He gave a loose shrug. "All right, if that's the way you want it."

"Only don't come here again," she said hastily, trying to think up a reason. "I . . . I work irregular hours . . . "

Ash had been studying her as she stumbled over the words and he appeared puzzled. All at once he leaned towards her and seized her wrist.

She dropped the cutters onto the tiled floor with a loud clatter. The sound vibrated in her ears like a musical instrument being badly played.

"What's the matter with you?" he asked suspiciously his eyes searching her face. "You seem agitated and very anxious to get rid of me. What are you up to?"

His touch was tying her nervous system in knots and she shook involuntarily. His very proximity had a weakening effect on her and she sensed all power drain from her legs.

He detected the subtle change in her and placed a warm hand under her chin, forcing her head up till her eyes gazed into his.

"Don't! Oh please don't," she moaned at this man who had caused her so much pain and unhappiness.

His other hand reached up to remove the single skewer-comb holding her hair in place. As it cascaded around her shoulders she cried, "I wish you'd stop doing that!"

His smouldering gaze ruthlessly toured her features. "You are still young and beautiful, Jillane," he murmured softly, barely audible. "As you were when I first saw you. In Scotland. What happened to us?" He brought his cheek to hers and she felt the faint scratch of stubble.

With superhuman effort she rallied her defences. "Stop it, Ash! It's all water under the bridge. Besides, this is neither the time nor the place. Can't you see that I want you to go?"

His reply was silky smooth with the hint of an underlying threat. "And I want to stay till I've found out why you want me to go."

"Oh you! You're exasperating, as always." She gave a short laugh. "It's quite simple. Matthew will be here in a moment . . . "

"Ah, so it is him!" He drew her towards him. "Frankly I shouldn't have thought he was your type at all."

"My type?" she echoed, wriggling to be free of him, in vain. "What do you know about my type?"

"Ah, I know!" His mouth curved as

it swooped towards hers. "You like a man who excites you."

"Oh, do I?"

"A man like me."

"Really?"

His lips were an inch away from hers and all her senses were on red alert. Her nose detected his distinctive cologne, her ears his quickened breathing. His touch was sending goose pimples racing up her arms.

His voice dropped to a new even huskier level. "Does Matthew kiss you like this?"

She twisted and turned for all she was worth but could not prevent him from carrying out his intention.

Her nerves were at breaking point as he jerked her closer into his arms. She felt the hard buttons of his jacket digging into her chest through the thin material of her T-shirt. As his lips eclipsed hers the impact sent a shock wave careering through her nerve centre. At once she was transported back through the years to those few heavenly days when they had lived together in the hotel in Scotland, before things had started to become complicated.

His kiss was impertinent, his lips moving teasingly over hers, feathering, tingling, until she felt dizzy from the thrill of it. Without meaning to, she slid her hands up over the leather jacket and onto his broad shoulders. Directly she realised what she was doing she tried to pull them away again but they seemed glued in place. And still the kiss went on.

She mustered up some stagnant hate for him. How dared he! Forcing himself in here and . . . Oh God! Would this abominable kiss never end!

Slowly he released her and she allowed her hands to slide to her sides.

"Well, does he?" he demanded.

She pushed her fingers through her hair and was aware her cheeks were flushed. "What? Who?"

"Matthew. Kiss you like that."

"No!" She hadn't meant to admit that. She cast round for something to justify her unguarded remark. "Because . . . he hardly kisses me at all." And she had not meant to divulge that either. By trying to make things better she had made them worse.

Ash looked askance. "I find that hard to believe, a sensual woman like you. How does he manage to keep his hands off you? I haven't met the man face to face but I've seen him and spoken to him on the phone. He doesn't come over as a wimp."

She kept her temper with difficulty. "You may think what you like, but because a man is sensitive it doesn't follow he's a wimp."

"I stand corrected."

They stared at each other, blue eyes and honeyed-brown in a clash of wills. Jillane knew her high colour gave her away. In the silence that lengthened between them in the quiet room, a small voice could be heard outside the open kitchen window.

"Mummy! Is it time for that programme about the polar bears?"

Jillane's face went from flushed to pale in rapid succession. She saw Ash cock his head and a puzzled expression crease his brow. In another moment he had crossed to the window and looked out.

"What the . . . ?"

Jillane glanced apprehensively towards the back door through which Pepper would step any moment.

"Please go!" She grabbed his arm.

He shook her away and stood his ground.

The little girl entered the kitchen carrying one of Jillane's handbags and a scrubbing brush. Her dungarees were covered with grass stains and her face was dirty from the chocolate bar she'd had after lunch. She'd lost the ribbon from her pony-tail and her hair was a black delightfully-tangled nest.

She gazed solemnly first at the stranger and then at the roses on the table before carrying on through to the sitting-room. At once the sound of the television floated out to them.

Jillane waited for all hell to break loose.

Ash's face was fast running out of expressions as he worked things out. Interest, bemusement, suspicion, calculation and finally conclusion.

He rounded on Jillane and, seizing her wrists in a savage grip, let out a cry like that of a wounded animal.

"You bitch!"

5

WITH a face like a thunderstorm Ash closed the door behind Pepper and ordered Jillane to be seated. She dropped into a chair at the kitchen table and motioned him to do the same, but he chose to remain standing.

"Right, start talking!" He grated out the words so angrily she flinched.

This was the moment she had been dreading more than any other — having to explain and justify her actions. It was no good her trying to deny Pepper was his daughter. With that hair and those eyes? He wasn't stupid and he wasn't blind. How was she to convince him without antagonising him further that she had behaved out of desperation?

Haltingly she began her story, starting with all the occasions when he had

110

neglected her. They sounded trivial from this distance in time but she forged ahead doggedly.

His expression was unfathomable. He was plainly shocked by his discovery but at pains to disguise the depth of his distress. However, when at last he spoke she was left in no doubt as to his opinion of her.

"You are a liar and a thief, Jillane. You have robbed me of the first five years of my daughter's life, the formative years I understand. I want to know what you intend doing to make amends."

She caught her breath painfully. "Amends?"

"I can assure you, you are not going to rob me of any more years." He thrust his chin forward in a familiar aggressive manner. "From now on I intend to take an active role in her upbringing and education and anything else of importance which crops up."

"And when are you going to find the time for that?" Jillane asked bitterly.

"I'll find time," he promised. "Don't you worry."

Jillane's heart sank. It was as she had feared from the start. She was bound to him by Pepper and there was to be no escape till the child was grown, perhaps not even then. Suddenly the years of Pepper's childhood, which had filled her with pleasurable anticipation, now looked bleak.

"Please, Ash, be reasonable," she protested. "We can't both run her life. It will be too confusing for her. I've coped pretty well up until now, if I do say so myself. Why don't you just let things go on as they are?"

"Oh no, you'd like that, wouldn't you?" His smile was chilling, not quite reaching his eyes. "You'd be able to tell her what a bastard I am! How I neglected you to run my business."

"I . . . wouldn't . . ."

"All right, what will you tell her when she asks after her father? As she will, any day now!"

Jillane chewed the inside of her

cheek. Pepper had already remarked puzzlingly on some children at school having fathers and others not. It was only a matter of time before she asked the main question. "I . . . shall tell her . . . " Jillane stopped. What would she tell her?

Ash answered for her. "That he's abroad? In prison? Dead?" His brows met. "Yes. You'd better say he's dead. Because, believe me, you'll have to kill him off, otherwise she's going to wonder why he doesn't love her enough to visit her."

Jillane hadn't thought that far ahead. It occurred to her that Ash was more sensitive than she had supposed. She wondered then if he had personal experience of such things. She knew he had been brought up by his father who was now dead.

He was speaking again. "Well, it won't come to that now. Because I'm here and she's going to know who I am." He moved towards the door. "It's best that we tell her together."

"And how do you propose to explain your absence till now?" asked Jillane, jumping up and grabbing his arm. "You're surely not going to tell her it's all my fault, for denying her existence . . . ?"

"No, I'm not going to do that."

Relief poured over her like soft summer rain. "Thank you!"

"Don't thank me!" His eyes glittered. "I'm not doing it for you! I am doing it to spare my daughter any unnecessary pain."

"I see."

He thought rapidly. "I think it will be best if we say I've been working abroad. We needn't go into any details. She'll accept it without question at her age."

"I'm still not convinced we should tell her anything," she replied stubbornly. Oh, why was he doing this? Why didn't he just go away and leave them alone? "This is just an ego trip on your part," she added spiritedly. "You want to win her affection. Then, when the novelty wears off, you'll go away again and I'll have to explain your absence."

He looked astounded. "My word! You do have a poor opinion of me. But you're wrong. I intend to stick around." He met her gaze defiantly. "If you won't help me tell her I shall tell her on my own."

He went out into the hall.

"Okay!" shouted Jillane, knowing she was beaten. She bounded after him. "Very well, we'll tell her together."

He let out the breath he had been holding and tucked her hand under his arm. "We'll make it a united front, show her we care for her as a team, a happy couple."

"Oh, I see." She turned her head to stare at him. "More lies?"

"What do you suggest then?" he snapped back. "We go in there battling it out? You in the blue corner, me in the red?"

"No, you're right." She hated admitting it but his plan was the only solution.

Although the television was on Pepper was not watching it. She sat on the edge of the settee looking preoccupied. She stood up as they entered and before either of them could speak asked in a frightened little voice, "Are you my daddy?"

"Yes," Jillane said. "How did you know?"

"I just knew." She stood still, staring with anxious eyes at Ash.

He bent down and spread his arms. "Come here, darling!"

Pepper hesitated for a moment and glanced at Jillane.

Jillane nodded.

A smile broke over Pepper's face and she flung herself, crying and laughing, into Ash's arms.

He appeared greatly moved and Jillane felt she was intruding on a most personal moment.

"Pepper." He savoured the name. "I like it. It suits you."

He sat on the settee and spoke quietly with the child, telling her he'd been abroad and asking her questions about herself. Jillane watched with decidedly mixed feelings. The two of them went well together and there was already an affinity between them. It was uncanny how even before Pepper had been given any idea of the stranger's identity she had known who he was.

Here was a side of Ash Jillane hadn't witnessed before and her fixed ideas about him were taking a knock. This gentleness, after the vile name he had called her, was muddling her mind. She saw how much the knowledge that the girl was his flesh and blood affected him and she felt guilty as hell. She had been terribly wrong, depriving him of those five precious years of Pepper's upbringing.

After a moment her conscience quietened a little and a rush of good sense returned. Ash hadn't changed. This was a new experience for him and he was tentatively feeling his way. He would soon get bored with the idea of being a father and then he would revert to type. She knew him. There was nothing with which to reproach herself.

All the same it was fascinating to witness him in this mood. And quite unnerving, with Pepper laughing at his jokes and he joining in.

The three of them had an early high tea together and Pepper told Ash about school. Afterwards she showed him her dolls. While Jillane washed up he read her a fairy story and presently helped put the excited child to bed.

Together they descended to the sitting-room to thrash out the demarcation lines of this armed neutrality.

However before either of them could get to grips with the realities Matthew arrived.

Jillane had forgotten all about him coming to dinner. At the sound of his footsteps outside the window she stared round in alarm.

She went to let him in. "I have a visitor."

He followed her to the sitting-room

and stopped dead at the sight of Ash who had risen to his feet from the armchair.

Matthew must have guessed who the visitor was but he said politely, "Oh, you're entertaining. I'll make myself scarce."

"No, don't go, Matthew," she called. "This is Ash Carey, my . . . " She stopped, too embarrassed to describe him as her husband. She didn't see him as such, although she realised with a sinking heart that she was going to have to get used to it, for Pepper's sake.

"Ash, this is Matthew Wyler," she finished.

The two men eyed each other warily as they shook hands. Matthew appeared unsure of himself and Ash's attitude was decidedly cool. Poor Matthew, thought Jillane, stepping innocently into this hornets' nest.

There was no way they could discuss anything now.

Ash solved the problem by inviting her to have dinner with him the following evening. She didn't see how she could get out of it.

Matthew watched him go down the path and climb into the Lotus. "So, that's him. I suppose he found out about Pepper?"

She gave him a brief resumé of their altercation.

"You'll probably tell me to mind my own business, but I'd go for a divorce if I were you." He shifted his feet uneasily. "That way it all becomes official and the court awards strict access. Otherwise you'll have him popping up whenever he feels like it."

"Why, yes, that's a valid point, Matthew. I'll bear it in mind. Thank you."

★ ★ ★

Jillane spent most of Sunday afternoon worrying what to wear for her impending meeting with Ash, taking outfits from her wardrobe, trying them on and discarding them. It was ridiculous. As if it mattered what she wore.

The fact was Ash made her nervous and she needed to feel confident about her clothes at least. Looking good meant feeling good and she'd be more able to keep up her end of the argument if she were well-dressed.

For argument there would be, she knew it as well as she knew the earth went round the sun.

She wanted to appear in something that wasn't too dressy, but wasn't too casual either, ideally a cross between a ball-gown and a tailored suit. Something which would make him sit up and take notice but not look as if she had gone to too much trouble. It seemed an impossible order.

Although he'd agreed to pick her up at eight it was a quarter to when he arrived.

Still undecided what to wear she was in her dressing-gown when she answered the door. He raised enquiring eyebrows but made no comment.

He looked handsome in a dark brown

suit and crisp white shirt. It was so easy for men, she thought irritably. But then he would always look just right no matter what he wore, from swimming trunks to evening dress.

Steady on, she warned herself. Thinking about him along those lines could get her into dangerous waters.

Vikki had already arrived to babysit and she gave Ash an admiring look as he entered the hall. "Oo, he's nice!" she said to Jillane out of the corner of her mouth.

"I take it you have no objections if I say goodnight to my daughter?" he asked.

"Go ahead," said Jillane. "She won't be asleep yet. As a matter of fact she's been waiting for you to come and refused to lie down."

She saw Vikki's eyes grow round with curiosity but did not enlighten her. It was a tricky situation to explain and would take time, which she didn't have just then.

"I'll get ready," she told Ash,

following him up the stairs and dashing into her bedroom. "Read her a story."

There was no time to dally. She threw on a crystal-pleated skirt of cornflower blue with a matching top, added a silver belt and slipped her feet into a pair of silver high-heeled shoes.

She always used make-up sparingly. A little foundation and a hint of blusher usually sufficed. Tonight she left off the blusher, sensing she was going to have enough of her own colour. The periwinkle blueness of her eyes needed no embellishment. She slashed a creamy rose lipstick across her mouth and sprayed her wrists generously with *Je Reviens*.

She was brushing her silky hair into an oaten curtain when she saw him in the mirror reflection leaning nonchalantly against her open door. She swung round so quickly her skirt floated out about her legs in a swirling blue haze.

He gave a low whistle. "You look gorgeous, Jillane." His voice vibrated, low and husky. "Perhaps we should stay in after all."

She shot him a look of censure before grabbing up her white evening jacket and silver bag and starting for the door.

As she drew level with him his hands shot out.

She shied away. "Don't . . . !"

But he was only relieving her of the jacket which he draped around her shoulders.

Downstairs, thoroughly disorientated, she gave a few unnecessary instructions to Vikki.

"Come on," said Ash impatiently. "I've got a taxi waiting."

He was making her feel guilty again. "All this time? You might have said."

He held the door of the cab for her and watched her slide her legs in.

"Not many women look elegant when they get into a low vehicle," he observed, climbing in beside her. "I'd forgotten you do."

She kept her eyes on the road ahead.

It looked as if he wasn't going to play fair and she needed to keep her wits about her to avoid falling at the first hurdle.

Apprehensive and not knowing what to say to him, she was relieved when he took out his mobile phone and began speaking to Hugo Brooking.

"Forgive me," he said, tucking the aerial back into the instrument and pocketing it. "I had to make contact with the company. Hanging around Denbridge to talk with you has eaten into my time."

No-one asked you to, she thought.

They stopped outside a restaurant on the outskirts of the town, a small intimate hostelry which looked expensive. She thought of his devious business tactics and wondered if this was a softening-up process. The thought amused her, because it wasn't going to work.

The head waiter, wearing elaborate livery, led them to a table by a window overlooking a floodlit lake. One glance at the menu showed Jillane that her first impression had been right. Trust him, she thought belligerently, trying to win points by flashing his money around.

He perused the menu. "How about a . . . ?"

"You order for me!" she muttered, determined not to be impressed. There was something personal about poring over a menu together and she would not give him that satisfaction. "Something small and low-caloried."

His eyes did a thorough tour over as much of her figure as he could see above the table. "You're not slimming!"

"No." She sipped the aperitif he had ordered. "But I prefer not to eat too much late at night."

The fact was she wasn't hungry. She was too keyed up even to think about food, which wasn't like her at all.

"Oh go on," he urged. "I seem to remember you like to gorge."

"I do not gorge! I have never gorged!"

"Oh, you know what I mean. Let's say you have a healthy appetite."

"Stop talking to me as if I were seventeen!" she hissed, keeping her voice low so the waiter would not hear her. "I am no longer your child bride."

His eyes did another exploration of her figure, dwelling on the firm swell of her breasts. "No, I can see that." He handed the menu to the hovering waiter and asked for two medium-rare steaks with side salads.

Jillane glanced round the restaurant. The diners looked well-heeled and she noticed the little covetous glances the women were giving Ash. He must be aware of them but he gave no sign of their interest and no encouragement. She remembered it was something she had always admired about him. He gave his sole attention to the woman he was with.

What did they see, she mused, these

rich women when they looked at him? She studied him as he studied the wine list. An attractive man of course. A man of authority — for assertiveness was written all over him. He was obviously used to having his orders carried out and head waiters held no alarm for him. Many women would find that irresistible. And then there was his sensual aura, an elusive promise contained in his eyes, his mouth, the tilt of his head . . .

"Have you quite finished?"

He was watching her in turn with a faintly amused expression and she was glad she hadn't used the blusher.

"I don't know what you mean," she said haughtily. How annoying being caught out in her appraisal. She dragged her gaze away from the sardonic glint in his eyes and made a show of fumbling in her bag for something.

She heard him chuckle and was reminded of times long ago. No-one chuckled quite so outrageously as him.

He ordered a bottle of vintage

Chateau Greysac to accompany the steaks and as soon as they arrived he broached the subject which had brought them together.

"Matthew thinks I should go for a divorce," she said without thinking.

At once Ash's eyes grew hooded. "So you discuss your most intimate secrets with the guy? Forgive me, I didn't realise you were on such close terms."

"Oh yes," she said blithely. "Matthew and I don't have any secrets." Well hardly any, she thought.

She returned his glare with a sweet smile.

"Well, I don't think divorce is the answer. It's hard for a child to come to grips with."

She thought again that he must speak from personal experience.

"What then?"

The Dover soles arrived and she watched the waiter prepare them on his little trolley. It gave her time to think. What was Ash up to? He sounded perfectly reasonable at the moment but she sensed he would lose his temper and turn nasty if he did not get his own way.

The wine waiter approached with a bottle of Sauternes Delaunay Freres. It was tasted, pronounced excellent and poured.

"What then?" she repeated when they were alone again. "Legal separation? That sounds just as bad."

"And it stops you from marrying Matthew." There was that sneer in his voice again. "You do intend to marry him?"

She decided on a flippant reply. "Not at the moment. I'm not into bigamy."

It was a mistake for he did not smile.

"Eventually?" he asked.

"Who knows? Perhaps!"

"I'd be obliged if you'd take this matter seriously."

"I am taking it seriously!" she exploded. "But you sound so pompous . . . "

"Thank you."

"I didn't mean . . . "

"I think you did."

The waiter was rigging up the stove for the Crepes Suzette and she transferred her attention to him.

Ash contained himself till they were half through the sweet course then he dropped his bombshell. "I've been on to my solicitor to see about setting up a trust for Pepper, to come into effect immediately."

Jillane was at once on the defensive. "I look after her very well. I have an excellent job. She wants for nothing."

"Have I said otherwise?" He arched his dark brows. "Pepper is my sole heir. Will she thank you one day, when she's old enough to understand, for keeping from her the obvious advantages of her inheritance?"

Jillane reluctantly conceded he was right. He had such a lot to offer. Darn him! She wasn't coming out of this very well. He held all the trump cards.

"Besides you cannot stop me," he

pointed out silkily. "However, I do not think it would be in anyone's best interests if we quarrel over custody of her."

Till that moment she had not for a moment considered the likelihood of his taking Pepper away from her, now she saw that it was all too possible. He was certainly capable of it. He was a ruthless man in his business dealings, why should she suppose he would not push any advantage home in the matter of his daughter's custody?

She felt cold suddenly, as if someone had dropped an ice cube down her back. How would a judge decide the matter if it came to court? Ash would have quite a case. His wife had walked out without an explanation, taking their child. Didn't that show she was deranged, m'lud, and not a fit person . . .

Well, she was not going to lie down and take it. She was prepared to fight for Pepper.

Incensed, she said, "You're acting

high-handedly as usual. Can't you understand, she's always been my responsibility and now suddenly you step in and start taking over."

He let that pass. "I've also made enquiries about a school . . . "

"Oh have you? She's only just started where she is."

He smiled blandly. "So it won't matter if she is uprooted."

Jillane decided to forego the offer of coffee and liqueurs. She wanted to get home to Pepper, who was becoming more precious by the minute.

"What's the hurry?" he asked, plainly exasperated with her. "You've got the babysitter."

He seemed anxious to keep her there at the restaurant. Why? As he sat there calmly, her fertile imagination started running haywire. What if . . . ? She stared at him in horror. What if he had arranged for someone — Hugo perhaps — to kidnap Pepper! That phonecall in the taxi could have been a code — to let him know the coast was clear.

"I want to go home!"

"All right, all right!" He beckoned the waiter. "No need to get hysterical." His eyes studied her face. "I think you're doing too much, working and bringing up a child . . . "

There! He was trying to find grounds for taking Pepper lawfully. For 'hysterical' read 'insane', for 'doing too much' read 'neglecting'!

"Stop it, Ash!" She leapt to her feet. "I know what you're doing. Well, it won't work, you know!"

"What won't? For heaven's sake calm down!" He paid the bill with his Diner's Card and rose also. Draping her jacket round her shoulders, he asked irritably, "What ever's got into you?"

She pushed past him and headed for the door, calling over her shoulder, "You think you're going to have me put away so you can . . . " She realised people were looking and closed her mouth. With her face aflame, she rushed into the foyer.

He followed her at a leisurely pace.

"I think I've got a good chance of succeeding, the way you're behaving." His words were clipped and she knew from past experience that he was furious with her.

He had every right to be. She was furious with herself.

"Wait there!" he ordered. "I'll phone for a taxi."

She watched him stride to one of the perspex hoods on the wall.

She grabbed a steadying breath. She hadn't meant to make a scene in public like that. It wasn't her style. And she had foolishly shown her hand, letting him know she suspected him, giving him time to make alternative arrangements . . .

She glanced quickly at him speaking into the receiver. That could be what he was doing now, warning Hugo that they were leaving early!

She ran outside, intent on getting her own cab. One was cruising round the corner. She ran forward, waving.

It stopped and the cabbie asked,

"Name of Carey?"

She felt Ash's hand on her elbow and was fairly pushed into the seat.

He closed the door and told the cabbie her address before turning to her. "Will you stop acting like a kid and tell me what's the matter?"

The 'kid' taunt brought her up with a start. All at once everything seemed so hopeless. She'd gone to pieces in front of all those witnesses and Ash was going to win custody by her default. She burst into tears.

"Don't take her away from me, please," she sobbed, clinging to his sleeve. "She's all I've got."

He stared at her in the dim light. "Take her away from you? God, Jillane! What sort of a monster do you take me for?"

She knew she was making things worse and playing right into his hands. At a loss to know what had come over her, she made a pathetic attempt to repair the damage. "I . . . don't think you're a monster."

He sat there staring straight ahead of him as erect and motionless as a totem pole, plainly too angry to risk saying anything he might later regret.

The moment they arrived at *Rose Villa* she flung herself out of the taxi while Ash was paying the fare. By the time he had completed the transaction she had found her key and was inside running along the hall.

Vikki must have been alarmed by the commotion and she appeared in the sitting-room doorway eating a chocolate bar.

Jillane stopped dead. Vikki hadn't been tied up and gagged then. Thank goodness!

"Oh Vikki, you're not . . . you haven't . . . "

Ash came in the front door. "Jillane! Stop this nonsense! Pull yourself together! You're being utterly ridiculous!"

Vikki stared openmouthed for a moment then discreetly went back in the room and closed the door.

Jillane just stood there as the eruptions taking place within her gradually subsided. As she came to her senses she was aware of Ash's eyes on her. She averted her own gaze and went up the stairs.

He followed her into Pepper's room. Jillane's panic evaporated completely when she gazed on the sleeping child.

She owed Ash an apology. "I'm sorry," she whispered. "My behaviour was unforgivable."

Tears were trembling on her lids again and he pulled her head onto his shoulder.

"You didn't really think I'd steal her, did you?" he murmured into her ear.

A sigh travelled through the length of her body. "No, I wasn't thinking straight. It was just the thought of losing her . . . "

He stroked her hair. "I know."

Pepper chose that moment to open her eyes. "Mummy, Daddy!" she said indistinctly. "It's a lovely dream." And she promptly went back to sleep again.

"There's the reason I would never try to steal her," muttered Ash, pulling Jillane out of the room and quietly closing the door. "She wants us both."

He stood still, the muted light from the landing lamp shedding a warm glow over his features. His hair looked densely black and his lashes cast spikey shadows on his gaunt cheeks. She gulped in a few shallow breaths.

Strangely, Hugo's words came to her. 'You must have loved him once.' Yes, she had loved him, to distraction. Ah, but was it really love? She'd been a girl of sixteen, unfamiliar with the ways of the world, and subsequent events had proved her vulnerability. Had she merely been enamoured with the idea of being in love? However, as they said in the song, no-one could take away from her the memories of those five heavenly days — before everything turned sour.

Unbidden, the painful memories crowded in too. Knowing he had married her because of her condition . . . never seeing him . . . the way he had deserted her just when she needed him . . . his outburst accusing her of deliberately . . .

"What are you thinking?"

She jumped. "What to wear tomorrow."

"Liar!"

She didn't contradict him.

"Well, I'd better be going."

"I'll get you a taxi." She was painfully aware of him, could hear his breathing, smell his cologne. She ached to be in his arms, be kissed by him. Her treacherous heart apparently had no pride.

"Thank you for the meal," she said, remembering the reason for it. "We haven't resolved the problem."

"It's late. Another time."

"But I . . . can't have you calling round all the time." She knew he wouldn't like it but it had to be said. "I need to know where I stand."

He *didn't* like it. A frown creased his brow. "From the looks you've been giving me I reckon I could come round

140

here any time I like and take up where we left off."

She bridled. "You most certainly could not!"

"And for that reason a divorce is not necessary," he went on.

"It most certainly is!"

"Really." He reached out and caught her hand. "Prove it!"

His other hand touched her breast and she gasped out loud. "Don't," she said weakly.

"Mrs Talbot!" Vikki called from downstairs. "Shall I ring for a taxi?"

Jillane welcomed the interruption and the excuse to escape. "I'll do it." She shook Ash off and went downstairs.

As she reached for the phone she realised that in a very short time the two of them would be alone. "Ash, would you like to share your taxi with Vikki?"

His expression as he descended the stairs was a revelation. Disappointment was uppermost, but there was also a hint of irony. Smiling at Vikki, he drawled, "It'll be a pleasure."

Jillane shot him a glance of triumph and picked up the receiver.

Vikki went to get her coat and Ash said, "Mrs Talbot? I suppose Pepper's called Talbot too?"

Jillane nodded. "It was the simplest thing to do."

His face was suffused with anger. "I won't have it," he growled. "I will not have my child called Talbot."

Vikki re-entered the room and the three of them talked generally for five minutes till there came a toot.

Jillane opened the front door.

Ash allowed Vikki to pass through first then he dropped a kiss on Jillane's cheek.

"Any time I like!"

6

THE following Saturday, because the good weather was holding, Jillane decided to take Pepper to Whitley Bay for the day. Directly Matthew discovered where they were going he offered to drive them to the coast.

Their first port of call was the main promenade to purchase a bucket and spade and three ice creams. Then they hired two deckchairs on the beach while Pepper paddled.

"I am very fond of you both," Matthew murmured, eyes closed. "You must know that."

"Yes." Jillane watched him warily.

"You know what I'm going to say next," he went on. "I want to marry you . . . " He turned his head to look at her and grinned sheepishly. "Oh, I know you've got to get a divorce first, but afterwards, when it's all over, I want you to be my wife."

"We'll see." She was relieved when Pepper came running up the beach asking to ride on the roundabout. She couldn't marry Matthew. He was a nice man but she didn't love him. Besides she wasn't planning on marrying again.

Ash was waiting for them when they returned to Denbridge in the early evening, his white Lotus parked outside *Rose Villa*, his expression displeased.

"Where have you been?" he asked irritably, getting out and coming over to them. "I've been coming and going all day in the hopes of catching you. It's inconvenient driving all this way and finding you out."

Pepper threw herself into his arms. "We've been to the seaside with Uncle Matthew, Daddy. I went on the roundabout. I rode in Cinderella's coach."

"Did you, darling?" He swung her round, his expression transformed. "I bet you were the prettiest Cinderella in the whole wide world."

She laughed shyly. "Oh, Daddy!" She held up a tiny pink teddy. "I won this on the hoopla."

"How clever of you!" And father and daughter stood grinning at each other.

Jillane watched them. They were so alike and they formed a mutual admiration society.

"Uncle Matthew helped me make a sandcastle," Pepper babbled on.

"Yes, I bet he did!"

Jillane glared at him.

"I can't afford to keep neglecting my business," he grumbled. "You might have let me know you planned to be out all day, Jillane. I left you a number where I can be reached. I'd arranged to take you both to a theme park."

"You can't expect me to phone you with every move I make," she replied briskly. "And I can't just drop everything to fall in with your plans. I suggest you phone me first before you make arrangements and get tickets for things."

He looked as if he might have more to say on the subject, but he noticed Pepper was listening, gazing up at him with adoring eyes, and said, "Well, I'll take you tomorrow."

"I'm working tomorrow," Jillane lied. She saw her daughter's crestfallen face. "You can take Pepper though."

"Great!" yelled Pepper.

"That's the idea," said Matthew after Ash had left. "Keep busy, be a moving target. The man has a cheek thinking you'll be available whenever he crooks his little finger."

Ash called for Pepper so early on Sunday morning they were only half way through breakfast. At the sight of him Pepper wanted to get down from the table, so he joined her for cornflakes and juice and they had a race to see who could finish first.

They went off down the path hand in hand and Jillane was forced to swallow a kingsized lump which had become wedged in her throat. All the evidence pointed so overwhelmingly to her having been wrong to take Pepper away after her birth. She had seriously miscalculated his reaction when she had assumed she was acting for the best. She hadn't known Ash would be so hurt. She resolved that when he returned at six o'clock she would convey to him how much she regretted everything.

But six o'clock came and there was no sign of them. To begin with Jillane thought little of it but when it was seven and they still had not returned her vivid imagination took over again. She had handed Pepper to a man who was ruthless when in the pursuit of what he wanted. And he wanted Pepper.

There was also the chance he might be trying to teach her a lesson to show her just what it felt like to have one's child taken away. Either way it was the behaviour of a dangerous man.

She rang Matthew and poured out her fears to him.

"Calm down," he told her. "I'll come at once."

"You've got it all wrong, my dear," he said when he arrived. "I don't think Ash is the type . . . "

"What do you know about it?" she snapped, almost demented with worry. "How clever of him to call early this morning. He's had all day to carry this kidnapping out. They've been gone eleven hours. They could be anywhere by now. Abroad even." She jutted her jaw. "I'm phoning the police."

She had picked up the receiver and was checking the number of the local police station on a list of emergency numbers on the wall, when she heard a car draw up outside. She craned her neck out of the window and saw Pepper, holding a bulging carrier bag, alighting from the Lotus.

Jillane banged the phone down and raced outside.

"Pepper, oh Pepper!" She pulled the girl into her arms. "Oh, God, I thought I'd lost you!"

Pepper demanded to be put down and ran to hold Ash's hand as he came round the car to stand beside her on the pavement. "But I was out with Daddy. You know I was. We saw the animals and the man let me feed the donkeys and we went on a big slide into the water and got wet and I went in a fairy cave and Daddy drove me round in a space ship and we saw the pirates and then Daddy took me to Macdonalds'." She held up the carrier bag and added breathlessly, "I've got lots of presents."

"Yes, it all made us a bit late," added Ash amiably. "Sorry if you were worried."

Jillane turned on him angrily. "Sorry? Oh, that's all right then. I've been out of my mind and all you can say is sorry . . ."

Ash looked taken aback. He gave Pepper a quick hug. "Run along indoors, there's a good girl." He watched her go then addressed Jillane.

"Would you mind not speaking like

149

that in front of Pepper? Look." He glanced at his chronograph. "We're just over an hour later than I said. Hardly reason to call out the guard." He cast a sarcastic eye at Matthew as he spoke.

"How dare you frighten me like that . . . !" Jillane continued hotly.

"Steady on! You're not making any sense. What did you think had happened?" Ash's eyes narrowed. "Oh, I see, that old story again." He regarded her scornfully. "That's your guilty conscience talking, my dear. We're not all like you."

She gaped at him. "Just what do you mean by that?"

"I think you know. Careful, Jillane, you're beginning to sound paranoic."

She closed her mouth with a snap. Then, "And another thing. You shouldn't buy her lots of presents . . . "

She was talking to thin air. Ash had spun on his heel and got back into his car. The engine sprang to life and roared noisily way.

"The man's got a temper all right," remarked Matthew as if for something to say.

He followed her inside where Pepper had arranged the contents of the carrier bag on the kitchen table. It was plain for all to see that the 'presents' consisted of cheap sales promotional giveaways — a cardboard Indian headdress, a slim colouring book, a plastic pencil case filled with crayons, a cut-out lion, a rubber snake and a balloon, all bearing the theme park's logo. Jillane felt very foolish indeed.

★ ★ ★

Flying a cargo of antique books to Stockton-on-Tees gave Jillane time to mull over the problem that was Ash Carey.

For the moment her scheme for keeping him at a distance was working. Every time he had phoned during the previous three weeks she had told him she was just on her way out. She had not prevented him from taking Pepper out at weekends but as far as she was concerned he was wasting his time trying to include her. She felt rather pleased with herself although at the back of her mind was a niggling doubt about how much of this kind of treatment he would take from her.

If she could just hold out a little longer, she reasoned, surely he would tire of the game and give up. His business was of prime importance to him, as she knew to her bitter cost, and he would not be able to neglect it indefinitely. Constantly driving to Denbridge from Derbyshire must be taking its toll. Why, she was surprised he had hung around for so long.

She returned to the airport to find the object of her musings, dressed in chino trousers and an oversized padded blouson, waiting on the tarmac.

"What do you want?"

"If the mountain won't come to Mohammed."

"Does Matthew know you're here?"

"Certainly." He grinned lazily. "He's not very pleased about it."

"What do you want?" she asked again.

"We have to talk."

"I thought we had talked."

"We discussed divorce, yes." He took her elbow as they walked across to the Wyler's Wings building. "But divorce is not what I want."

"Wait a minute!" She shook his hand away and turned to face him. "It's what I want."

"Pepper needs two parents. Who better than us, her natural parents?"

"You're not suggesting . . . ?"

"Hold your horses! Let's talk the matter over reasonably."

"Reasonably?" she scoffed. "You talk and I listen, you mean?"

He breathed deeply. "When I insist Pepper needs the two of us as parents I don't mean we have to live together again as man and wife . . . "

"Well, thank goodness for that."

His eyes narrowed to honeyed slits.

"No child likes knowing their parents have split up. We don't need to involve the courts. You carry on looking after her and we can all meet up regularly to take her on family outings. I'll be 'working away' the rest of the time."

"Ye-es." It sounded a good idea but he was doing it again. Riding roughshod over any opinions she might have and taking it for granted she would agree to everything he suggested.

She tried to assert herself. "It won't be very nice if she hears us arguing."

"Why should we argue?" His eyebrows lifted innocently. "We both want what's best for her. Our own differences can be shelved for the comparatively short periods we shall be together. Besides arguments over Pepper should no longer arise." He smiled disarmingly. "Well, what do you say?"

It did seem to be the answer. "I don't know . . . "

"Don't you think you owe me something?" His expression was hard and unrelenting suddenly. "After keeping

154

her very existence from me all this time?"

"I suppose so." She sighed. "Yes, of course I owe you something. I know I can't make it up you but I really do want to try."

"That's settled then." Ash lightly touched Jillane's hand. "There's no need for you to keep hiding from me. I'm a busy man. When I get back to Derbyshire tonight I've got the annual general meeting to attend. And in a few days' time I'm off to a trade fair. It would be helpful if you would cooperate. I can't go through this rigmarole every time I want to speak to you."

She lowered her gaze. "I'm sorry."

He cleared his throat noisily. "Now we've settled things I want to take you and Pepper to the theatre. Next Saturday. There's a children's matinee at . . . "

"I'll see what we're doing . . . " she interrupted, gripped by panic. So soon? Had she capitulated too readily?

"I mean, we might have something planned . . . with Matthew . . . "

"Cancel it!"

"Will you stop ordering me about?"

"Am I ordering you about?" he asked wide-eyed. "I thought I was helping. I could have been very difficult about all this, you know. I could have made a fuss and taken you to court."

She looked up at him sharply.

He wore a grim expression. "I could have had Pepper taken away from you . . . "

She bridled. "On what grounds?"

"You must be guilty of a whole string of offences," he replied, ticking them off on his fingers. "Keeping a child from its rightful father. Registering a child under an incorrect name. Making false statements to the Department of Employment." His hooded gaze taunted her. "Need I go on?"

She froze. It was as if he was warning her what he could do if she did not come to heel. What he would be prepared to do in fact.

"Having me thrown into prison isn't going to further your plan to present Pepper with two united parents."

"You're right. And I hope it doesn't come to that." He smiled but the underlying edge of menace left her in no doubt as to his intention to have his way.

Silently she acknowledged her precarious position. He had her exactly where he wanted her. One false move and she lost Pepper. It was a form of blackmail.

He was studying her face as intently as though he were memorising every detail for further reference. His scrutiny made her hot and bothered and not a little self-conscious. As his eyes almost touched her, like a flickering fire, she drew short of breath and shivered involuntarily.

At once his eyes held concern. "Cold?"

"No." They had reached the shadow of the Wyler building. She hitched her tote bag higher on her shoulder. "Well . . ."

"How about the trip to the theatre on Saturday?"

"That will be fine," she said tight-lipped.

His hand shot out to capture her chin. "Cheer up, my dear, it's not the end of the world. I shall be on my best behaviour."

Oh yes, he could be nice to her now he'd got his way, she thought, and cursed herself for not standing up to him. Why did she always feel so young and gauche when she was in his presence? She should have remained firm and called his bluff. He had already decided they should appear on good terms for their daughter's sake and a court case would not have served his purpose. She could have pleaded a previous engagement and forced him to postpone the theatre trip.

"I'm glad we've come to an amicable arrangement," he murmured smoothly. "That wasn't too difficult, was it? We don't always have to turn it into a shouting match. Let's be civilised."

She opened her mouth to protest. Then shut it again. She had nothing to add.

"That's right," he noted dryly. "Don't say anything. Actions speak louder than words." And before she knew what was happening he had bent his head to kiss her full upon the mouth.

She backed away, her face bright pink. "Why did you do that?"

He gave a shrug so loose his arms appeared to be unconnected to his shoulders. "Because I wanted to. You're a beautiful woman, Jillane. Beautiful women should be kissed."

"That's no answer," she muttered. "I'd be grateful if you'd leave me alone in future."

"Oh? Would you?" he asked. "You'd like me to leave you alone?"

"That's what I said."

"Suppose I don't want to?"

"That's too bad."

His cool palms were a shock to

her burning cheeks as he caught her head between his hands. She sagged against him, acknowledging her body's clamouring for his mouth, needing it as she had never needed anything. Her brain might flinch from the idea but it could not deny the compulsion contained within herself.

His lips began feathering the sensitive flesh in the hollows of her throat.

"No!" Her protest was hardly more than a whisper.

It was muffled by his lips moving hungrily over hers, forcing them apart. Powerless to resist, she felt dizzy. Elation was rushing headlong through her veins and all she knew was the pressure of his lips, the hard structure of his frame, the feel of his fingers sifting through her oaten tresses.

His hand came up to fondle her body. As she awoke to his caresses she felt the flame she had thought dead, rekindled. She sighed, liking what he was doing and despising herself for her liking. She moaned softly.

He thrust her away and his mouth curved insolently. "Now don't let's have any more talk of you wanting me to leave you alone."

"Oh! You!" She raised her hand to slap his hateful face but he stalled her deftly by catching her wrist.

"Temper."

Frustration welled up inside her, closely followed by humiliation. He had brought her to the edge of desire and reduced her to a pulp with seemingly no effort at all.

Just to demonstrate he could.

She turned on her heel and fumbled her way into the office.

Matthew was speaking on the phone. He threw her a grin which died when he saw her expression of abject misery.

She sprawled in an armchair and mentally re-ran her encounter with Ash. This united front idea wasn't going to work. Not if he was going to behave like that every time they met. She would be a nervous wreck in no time. She could still feel the imprint of his lips and thought he might have branded her.

She took a small hand mirror from her bag and studied her reflection. Not a mark on her. But her cheeks were flushed and her eyes unusually bright.

Slowly she calmed down. They wouldn't be meeting all that often. He had a business to run and Pepper had to go to school. She brightened. The little girl would be with them whenever they met, acting as a sort of chaperone. There would be no repetition of this day's outrageous performance.

Matthew had finished his call and was watching the expressions flitting across her face. "You saw him then."

She got up and perched on the edge of the desk, swinging one leg angrily. "He won't even entertain the idea of a divorce. He wants us to pretend to Pepper that we are an old married couple."

"But you don't have to agree to that," Matthew pointed out. "You can get a divorce without his permission on the grounds of unreasonable behaviour . . . "

"That's just it. I can't," she explained gloomily. "I'm the one who's behaved unreasonably. If I don't play ball he'll have Pepper taken away from me."

"The monster!" Matthew rose from his chair. "He actually said that?"

"As good as."

"But . . . he can't . . . "

"He can." Her shoulders drooped as she contemplated the hopelessness of the situation. "Ash can do anything he puts his mind to."

Matthew put his arm round her trembling shoulders. "Nonsense! He's not Superman. My dear, you have allowed yourself to be brainwashed by this man."

"You don't know him like I do."

"I know the type," he said wryly. "Used to throwing their weight about. But you don't have to fight him alone any longer. You've got me now."

She smiled wanly at him through a sudden mist of unshed tears. "I know, Matthew. I'm grateful, really I am."

163

He sighed. "You've got to get your marriage sorted out, you know."

She swallowed hard. "Yes, I can see that."

There was a pause as if he were plucking up the courage to broach a delicate subject.

"From what you've told me, I'd say you weren't legally married."

"What!"

"You said it wasn't . . . consummated, therefore you could apply for an annulment."

"But . . . we have a child."

"She was conceived before the marriage."

Jillane considered this suggestion. "I couldn't do that to Pepper."

"No, well, perhaps not."

She thought for several moments. "Do you suppose Ash has realised this?"

"Bound to have."

Was that why he seemed so keen to cement their relationship? To stop her going for an annulment? She shivered.

"Remember," Matthew said, "an annulment would be simpler than a divorce." He added hesitantly, "Er . . . if non-consummation still applies, that is."

"Of course it still applies!" she answered hotly.

"Well, make sure you give him no opportunity to alter the situation."

"Don't worry!"

* * *

Ash's white car appeared outside punctually at two o'clock on Saturday afternoon.

Pepper, dressed in her red party frock, had been ready for ages and stood at her mother's bedroom window anxiously watching the road.

"He won't come any sooner for all your fretting," said Jillane easing herself into a close-fitting black two-piece which she was teaming with a silk camisole top of sapphire-blue.

"He will! I wish him here!" The

child laughed excitedly and clapped her hands as there came a toot. "And here he is!"

She flew down the stairs while Jillane finished dressing.

She could hear them laughing as she descended. They were unaware of her and she saw he had brought a toy monkey. The wrapping paper was all over the floor and Pepper was cuddling the toy while Ash looked on benignly. He appeared so proud, so full of love that Jillane caught her breath painfully.

"Mummy, Mummy! Look!" cried Pepper glimpsing her standing outside the door. "Daddy gave him to me."

"He's lovely."

Ash turned his attention to Jillane. "You look beautiful."

"Thank you." She thought he looked pretty good himself in a Prince of Wales check jacket and dark trousers.

He kissed her cheek in an absent-minded way and made no reference to their former stormy parting.

"I got this for you, Jillane." He held out a box containing a brilliant-blue orchid. "It will match the blouse you're wearing."

"Hm, very clever of you." She took the pearl-headed pin attached to the stem and secured the exotic bloom to her jacket.

"Not that clever," he confessed. "I figured it would at least match your fascinating eyes." He peered hard at them. "No, it's a poor second."

They got their coats and went outside to climb into the car, Pepper strapped in the narrow seat in the back, Jillane sitting beside Ash.

The theatre show was the Shakespearean play *The Tempest*, especially adapted for children. Pepper loved it — and so did Jillane.

"What ever made you think of it?" she asked Ash during the interval. "I didn't realise she was old enough to appreciate the Bard."

He looked pleased with himself. "Always give them something just that little bit beyond them and see them stretch to reach it."

They bought the promotional books and puzzles in the foyer then Ash drove them to Macdonald's for quarter-pounders and chocolate shakes.

Jillane thought he looked like an overgrown kid as he chased the last of the milk round the bottom of the beaker with his straw.

Pepper fell asleep on the way home and Ash carried her indoors where he gently woke her.

She put her thumb in her mouth and smiled up at him. "Hello, Daddy. I love you."

He seemed overcome for a moment and at a loss for words. Gently he kissed the top of her dark head then carried her up the stairs to her bedroom.

Jillane wondered how she was going to get rid of him. She needed a diversion. She went into the bathroom and locked the door then noisily ran the shower.

She took her time showering and

also washed her hair. He must have taken the hint because she heard the front door close and his footsteps on the path outside.

Dressed in her bathrobe, her hair in a towel, she ran lightly down the stairs and stopped. Ash was reclining on the settee. His eyes were closed but he wasn't asleep. The moment she entered he opened them.

Why hadn't she remembered how devious he could be?

He stood up. "What silly game are you playing, Jillane?" he demanded. "Couldn't you wait until I had gone before you took a shower? Is it too much to ask you to at least behave civilly?"

To hide her confusion, she gave her hair a brisk rub with the towel. "I thought it was Pepper you came to see. You can't expect me to put myself out for you more than I have to. I've already given up my afternoon for you."

She saw his nostrils flare and knew

she'd said the wrong thing. It was a mistake to risk antagonising him. He held all the aces. Besides her words, uttered in self defence, sounded mean to her ears.

"I'm much obliged to you for your time," he hissed. "It must have been purgatory having to spend the whole afternoon with me but you've only yourself to blame. If you'd been a decent sort of person and not kept my daughter from me you wouldn't be in this awkward position now." His eyes glittered like steely points of light. "You don't seem to realise the enormity of what you've done. You're not even sorry . . . "

"I am sorry . . . for keeping Pepper a secret," she burst out. "I thought I was acting for the good of all concerned. I honestly didn't think you would want to bother yourself with either of us."

He seized her wrist. "I don't know what gave you that idea."

"You did! You were never around.

I had the distinct impression I was in the way."

His eyes clouded with anger. "I had work to do that was vital. I thought I'd explained all that to you. I thought you understood. God! You couldn't have been that stupid!"

"You always said I was too young!" She flinched as his fingers bit into her flesh. "I didn't know you really meant I was stupid."

He was silent for a long time, breathing deeply. She quaked, not daring to take her eyes off him for a moment.

His glance changed subtly to become sardonic and he drawled, "You're right. I shouldn't have neglected you." He lifted one eyebrow. "Perhaps I can make it up to you some time. Now perhaps?"

The grip on her wrist loosened and he placed his other hand against her cheek. When he spoke again his voice was low and throbbed with intimate undertones. "There is an easy way of settling our differences."

For a moment she was at a loss to know what he was driving at. Then all at once his message became clear. She screamed her answer. "No!"

He adopted a silky tone. "But you are my wife."

"In name only," she retorted.

He cradled her gently in his arms. "We can put that right in no time at all."

Her body went rigid. "No!"

The word was hardly spoken before she suffered the erotic assault of his mouth coming down firmly on her own.

She struggled futilely, jerking her head this way and that but one of his hands was in the small of her back and she was trapped by the sheer power of him.

She was not fooled by his show of passion. This was no loving kiss between husband and wife. It was designed as a lesson to show her who was in control of the situation. Well, she would not be shown.

Keeping her lips tightly compressed to stop the invasion of his tongue, she kicked him hard on the shin with her bare heel.

He threw her from him and swore under his breath. She fell backwards to sprawl on the settee and her robe gaped open, exposing her white breasts and thighs.

He stood over her, his eyes drinking in her nakedness, his breath noisily vibrating round the room.

She frantically pulled the edges of the robe together. "Get out!"

He blinked and turned, then without a backward glance, did as she demanded.

Blind fury had paralysed her limbs and she remained on the settee for long moments. Another evening like this and she would be a total wreck.

7

"I'VE missed five of her Christmasses," Ash shouted. "She's coming to Derbyshire!"

He had returned Pepper from the skating rink and thrown his bombshell into Jillane's lap.

"What if I've already made my own arrangements?" she asked, ransacking her brains for a viable excuse. "Dorlene married again, you know. She and her new husband live in Malta. Last year she invited us out there. We had a marvellous time. Pepper loved it . . ."

Ash gripped her shoulders. "You still don't seem to realise how lenient I am being with you, Jillane." His eyes appeared to contain sparks of fury. "If I choose to I could have Pepper taken away from you."

She brought her arms up and

174

knocked his hands away. "You just try!"

They faced each other, breathing deeply, like warring animals.

He said, "The courts would look on my claim favourably."

"On what grounds, pray?"

"I believe there's some law about depriving a parent of a child. I'll get my solicitor to look it up. Then, as I said before, there's your state of mind."

"My . . . ?"

"One wonders if a fit person would act as you have done. Whether it is safe to leave a child in your doubtful care . . . "

He never got any further for she raised her hand and hit him as hard as she could across the cheek. The sound of flesh on flesh echoed round the kitchen. He barely flinched.

"How dare you!" she shouted, seeing the angry stain marking his cheek. "I'd kill you . . . !"

Once again he held her shoulders. "Calm down, Jillane. We don't need to keep having this argument. I was merely pointing out the various ways and means for getting control of Pepper if I had a mind to." His eyes were cold steel now. "Or was driven to it."

Her heart was racing from the sheer fright he had given her. She opened her mouth to speak but no sound came.

"So it seems a reasonable request to ask to have her for Christmas. You too, of course. Pepper wouldn't like it without you."

Slowly she grew calm. "Is that wise? Not so long ago we were speaking of a divorce. Wouldn't that prejudice it, living together under the same roof?"

"Divorce? I thought I'd made it clear. There will be no divorce. If we are to put on a united front for our daughter's sake a divorce is out of the question."

His words dealt a final death knell to her dreams of a quick settlement of their differences and a quiet life away from him.

"Look, I'm going to Switzerland

for two weeks," he said. "It's time-consuming having to keep driving to Denbridge from Derbyshire and I've been neglecting my business of late, but this is an important conference which can't be postponed. I shall be back a few days before Christmas and I want to get it settled now. So how about it?"

At once an image of his home brought to flood memories of her short time in that beautiful mansion and how unhappy she had been. "I'll have to think about that." But she knew she was beaten.

★ ★ ★

With Ash at the wheel of the Lotus, they arrived at the mansion during the morning of Christmas eve. Winter had set in with a vengeance by now and there was a thin coating of snow on the roads.

As they swept in through the wrought iron gates, Jillane couldn't help recalling the first time she had done so. He'd been at the wheel then too and she had been heavily pregnant. She had been hopeful, despite all the threatening done by her father, that Ash might after all have married her because he loved her. But the separate rooms and his long absences had put paid to all that.

Grasslands was a picturesque Elizabethan house standing on a hill overlooking a wooded valley. Stone-built and gabled it had twelve bedrooms, most of which had splendid views of the gardens falling away in lush terraces towards the village of Palmly nestling below.

Mrs Oliver, the housekeeper, was on the steps waiting to greet them. Fiftyish, she was a thin lively woman, all knees and elbows. She fussed over Pepper exclaiming how like her father she was and said how pleased she was to see Jillane again.

Jillane gave the woman a hug and wondered what Ash had told the staff. As far as they knew she had disappeared after losing the baby.

"I told them the truth," he said later when she asked how he wanted her return explained.

"Oh dear. I expect they hate me."

"Give me some credit," he sneered. "I told them you were suffering from post natal depression at the time and didn't know what you were doing."

That was something, she supposed, feeling humbled.

He said, "Perhaps it *is* true. I'm willing to give you the benefit of the doubt."

Inside the front door was a fifteen foot Christmas tree hung with lights and decorations, its base heaped with presents.

Ash saw Jillane's look of disapproval. "They're not all for Pepper. Some are for the staff." He smiled fondly at his daughter. "I'm having great fun making sure your Christmas is just right."

The child knelt by the tree and her voice filled with wonder. "Daddy! It's lovely!"

He grinned at Jillane and murmured, "Don't take this away from me."

She found she had another lump in her throat.

He whispered, "Do you mind if I provide Father Christmas's present?"

"Be my guest," she croaked.

She was thankful to discover she hadn't been given her old quarters but a large room at the rear of the house overlooking the kitchen gardens. The *en suite* bathroom contained a bath and a shower cubicle and her heels sank into the incredibly-thick pile of the carpet. Pepper was next door. She didn't know where Ash was and didn't ask.

After lunch Ash left to go to his office in Chesterfield taking Pepper with him. Jillane had some last minute shopping to do so she borrowed the estate Jeep and drove it into Bolsover.

She bought a bottle of sherry for Mrs Oliver and several sets of toiletries for the rest of the staff. There were a lot of them and she did not want to miss anyone. Ash's present caused the most trouble. After a good deal of thought she chose an electronic backgammon set for him. She signed the card 'Luv from Pepper and Jillane'.

When she returned to the house Ash's Lotus was parked out front. She opened the door to find him on his knees placing more packages beneath the tree.

He looked up and grinned guiltily.

Carol-singers called after dinner and were invited in. Pepper was allowed to stay up to listen to them before being sent off to bed in readiness for the great day tomorrow.

Ash invited Jillane into his study for a nightcap. The room was just as she remembered it, dark-panelled with leather armchairs and a massive desk, the real fire in the grate reflected in a glass cabinet filled with the various trophies he'd won for rugby and water sports.

He held up a bottle of cherry brandy. "This do?"

She nodded and wandered round the room. "Are you still interested in water sports?" she asked idly.

The ruby-coloured liquid in the glass he handed her caught the glow of the fire. "I'm interested but I don't have time to participate these days."

"That's a pity." She dropped into a chair beside the fire. "You were good."

He remained standing, staring into a large brandy balloon. "Yeah! Water sports brought us together."

Not wanting to be reminded of such things, she knocked back the warming liquid. "I think I'll turn in."

He opened the door for her and stared at her mouth as if wondering whether he should kiss her or not.

She hoped he wouldn't.

He decided against it and instead gave a little nod. "Don't worry," he said, reading her mind. "This is Pepper's week. I shall be on my best behaviour to ensure there's no friction between us."

Getting ready for bed, she hoped Ash would keep his promise. She considered locking the door but daren't in case Pepper, waking in a strange bed, might be frightened and need to come looking for her in the night.

The next thing she knew it was morning. Very early morning if the coldness were anything to go by.

Someone had switched on her bedside lamp and she saw it was just after six.

She slid out of bed to reach for her wrap and almost fell over Pepper squatting on the rug playing with an exquisite dolls' house with transparent walls.

"Look, Mummy, what Father Christmas brought me." Her voice was filled with wonder. "See, there are little tables inside and chairs and . . . everything!"

"Yes, I see, it really is magnificent." Jillane crouched down beside her. "How did you drag it in here?"

"Easy. It's not heavy."

Jillane tilted the side and discovered it was made of fibreglass. "I've never seen anything like it." She picked up one of the tiny chairs. "It looks like fairy furniture."

"Anybody up?"

Ash, clad in a striped towelling dressing gown, leaned on the door jamb.

Pepper ran over the carpet to him. "Look, Daddy, look what I've got!"

He bent to kiss the top of her head. "Happy Christmas, darling!"

He switched on the fire and all three knelt down beside the dolls' house.

Jillane said, "It's beautiful and so unusual. I wonder where Father Christmas got it."

"Probably in Switzerland," said Ash. "I believe he does a lot of his shopping there."

"Oh Daddy." Pepper laughed. "You are funny!"

After he went away they showered and dressed then went downstairs for breakfast.

Later the staff crowded round the tree in the hall for the distribution of the presents. Even those who lived out were in attendance and the room rang with noisy conversation.

"You're spoiling her," said Jillane goodhumouredly as Pepper's pile of toys, books, games and clothes grew.

He murmured softly so that no-one else would hear, "Only making up for lost time."

He opened the package containing the backgammon set she and Pepper had given him and kissed their cheeks in turn. Then he bent to pick up a long slim packet wrapped in gold-coloured paper bearing Jillane's name.

She was surprised. He'd already given her a silk nightie and negligee set and an expensive selection of Chanel No. 5 toiletries.

Her fingers shook clumsily as she pulled the ribbon undone and saw the Tiffany logo. She was aware of his and the others' eyes on her and hoped he hadn't bought her the crown jewels!

She lifted the lid to gape at a single rope of pearls.

He took the necklace from her trembling fingers and fastened it around her neck. A glance in the mirror over the mantle showed how well the pearls complemented her fair skin in the vee of her blue angora sweater. She wanted to say she couldn't accept such a gift, but not in front of everyone. Touching the pearls reverently she said, "They're beautiful. Thank you."

As she turned back to him he caught her shoulders and kissed her full upon the mouth. There came a murmur of approval and a stray burst of applause.

They had a traditional Christmas dinner with all the trimmings then the three of them wrapped up warm and went for a walk over the estate, a couple of red setters belonging to the gardener loping along with them.

The landscape was bleak, the firs burdened with snow and the sky leaden, hinting at more to come. Every now and then a blood-red sun showed itself through the clouds, sending long shadows across the fields and reminding them of the shortness of the winter's day.

While Pepper ran ahead with the dogs, Jillane and Ash walked side by side, hands pocketed.

Directly Pepper was out of earshot Jillane said, "I don't want to appear ungrateful but I can't accept the pearls. They're far too valuable. What ever possessed you to buy them?"

"They've been in my safe for five years," he said, staring ahead of him. "I bought them to give you when our baby was born."

She felt a stab of remorse somewhere in the region of her heart.

"So you see they belong to you, in a way." He took one hand from his jacket pocket and gripped her elbow. "Please accept them. I want you to have them, as a token of my appreciation for Pepper."

She didn't know what to say. It would sound churlish if she still insisted on refusing the gift. She decided to say nothing, wear them over the holiday, but leave the pearls behind on his desk when she left.

After tea they played games with the resident staff and the following day they went into Chesterfield to see *Aladdin*. Jillane was amazed to hear Ash shouting out the traditional responses to the actors.

Later, after Pepper had gone to bed, a few of Ash's friends and business colleagues called round in response to an invitation for drinks. Jillane recognised some of the people who had been playing croquet at the hilltop retreat. Sheridan and Hugo were also there, the latter accompanied by a pretty girl of about twenty.

He eyed Jillane devilishly as she stood unawares under the mistletoe in the hall and swiftly took advantage of the situation to kiss her. Not to be outdone Sheridan kissed Ash.

The woman was dressed in a white flying suit with silver buckles and, with her auburn hair drawn to the top of her head allowing a cluster of ringlets to hang down, looked stunning.

They spread themselves in the comfortable armchairs in the sitting-room while Ash poured the drinks.

Hugo sat next to Jillane. Wearing a told-you-so expression on his boyish face, he whispered, "There! You're glad now I brought you two together again, aren't you? It was all for the best. You should see Ash in the office. He's a changed man these days. Well, you must have noticed."

She raised her eyebrows mockingly. "Really! I can't say I have."

"Oh yes, he's much more relaxed."

"I'm glad one of us is."

The talk was general, they played cards and backgammon and sang carols. Altogether it was a very pleasant evening, Jillane decided.

But she felt uneasy in Sheridan's presence. She had always been in awe of the beautiful woman and resented her involvement with Ash. The two went a long way back. Sheridan would probably be Mrs Carey by now if

Jillane hadn't tricked him into marrying her instead. And yet the woman did not appear to bear her any ill will. That was the baffling part. Perhaps she was biding her time, waiting till he got this 'father thing' out of his system and came back to her. It might take a long time, mused Jillane. She herself had thought it a temporary aberration to begin with, now she wasn't so sure.

"That went very well," said Ash later as he and Jillane went upstairs.

He held her hand loosely and she cast a wary glance in his direction. His answering smile warmed her like the first sun of summer and she couldn't help but bask in it.

"Jillane," he murmured when they reached the landing. "I know I promised but . . . "

As if pulled by magnets she went into his arms to receive a batch of hungry little kisses, submerging her once more in the heady aura of him.

"Darling, I want you."

His hands were caressing her body

sending aching tremors snaking through her. Her loins seemed on fire and a low tortured moan escaped her. She sank her head against his shoulder, wanting him, and wondering how they had got to this stage so quickly.

All at once he was propelling her along the corridor towards her bedroom, taking her silence for acquiescence.

"Wait!" she cried, needing time to think.

"No more waiting." He opened the door.

"Daddy!"

Ash swore under his breath.

A sleepy-eyed Pepper came stumbling along the corridor dragging a panda by the foot. "I dreamed you went away again, Daddy."

Ash fixed his gaze on Jillane. "Well, that's one dream that will never come true." He picked the child up in his arms and carried her back along the corridor. "Daddy is here to stay."

Jillane escaped into her room and turned the key. She would unlock it later, before she got into bed, to give Pepper access, but for the moment it was a safeguard against his charisma and her own weakness.

It was a blessing Pepper had intervened just then. In another moment it would have been too late. It was all very well surrendering to her basic desires in the heat of the moment but what about the consequences? In return for gratifying her momentary needs she would have compromised her independence, which meant a great deal to her after all she had been through. She didn't want to love him. She didn't want to risk all that hurt ever again. She was a survivor and intended to remain one.

He and Pepper were already at breakfast when she got downstairs.

Ash threw her an intimate little smile, which she ignored.

As she mulled over the extravagant choices on the sideboard, she asked Pepper, "What was all that about a dream?"

The child muffled a giggle with her

hand. "Daddy said it was because I had chocolate before I went to bed."

"Did you? Have chocolate."

"Shush!" said Ash in a stage whisper. "Do you want to get me into trouble?"

Jillane frowned at him. "Oh, you didn't!"

"Only a small piece. And she cleaned her teeth afterwards." He held his arms over his head as if to ward off an attack. "Don't be angry!"

"Well." She hid a smile. "Just so long as it doesn't happen again."

"Oh it won't." He performed a sloppy kind of salute. "Honest injun."

Pepper was convulsed and Jillane had to admit they were on the same wavelength. Pepper had grown mentally in the few weeks Ash had been around. If only she were certain of his motives concerning herself.

Ash had promised to take Pepper to the Robin Hood Experience at Nottingham but just as they were about to leave the house a representative of Carey International phoned with some news which made him look grave.

"I'm sorry, young Pepper." He ruffled her hair. "I'm needed at the Chesterfield plant. We'll have to postpone our visit."

"That's all right, Daddy."

"It's not all right," grumbled Jillane reminded of past occasions when he had neglected her for the business. "Can't they leave you alone, even over Christmas?"

"This is slightly different. It's . . . "

"Oh, I've no doubt you have a wonderful excuse, but I don't want to hear it," she snapped. "You promised Pepper. This week belongs to her, you said."

He glared at her for a moment then addressed Pepper again. "I know I promised, but this really is something that I have to deal with personally. Do you understand?"

She put her arms round his neck as he bent towards her. "'Course I do."

They followed him into the hall and

watched him pull on his sheepskin jacket.

"Shan't be long. We'll do Robin Hood tomorrow."

"Stop worrying, Daddy."

He smiled at her, ignored Jillane totally and left.

"I think we'd better pack a few things ready for going home the day after tomorrow," said Jillane. "I hope we can find some boxes to pack all your presents in."

"Aw, have we got to go? Can't we live here?"

Jillane's heart seemed to turn over. It was what she had been dreading, Pepper getting to love the place and wanting to stay on. They should never have come.

"Don't be silly, darling. Daddy doesn't live here all the time. *Rose Villa* is our home and he knows where to find us there. What about your friends? And my job? Don't you think I should go back to it?"

"Suppose so," muttered Pepper.

195

They went upstairs to their bedrooms but Jillane was restless.

Leaving Pepper playing with her dolls' house she walked slowly through the house, wondering if she would ever be rid of the bitter memories — the room she had been given while she awaited the birth; the window on the landing from which she had watched so many times as Ash had driven away with Sheridan; the library where she had lied to him about the stillbirth.

Ash was in a melancholy mood when he returned to the mansion and he shut himself in his study for a considerable time with orders not to be disturbed.

After lunch his buoyancy returned and he played a rough and tumble game with Pepper, rolling around on the carpet pretending to be a wild animal. Growls from him and squeals of laughter from her echoed through the house.

Jillane left them to it and went to the large warm kitchen to see if she could help the cook with dinner. Mrs

Oliver was making soup from turkey leftovers and Jillane offered to make the croutons. After that she prepared the vegetables to accompany the fish and generally made herself useful.

"I was sorry to hear you'd been ill, Mrs Carey," said the woman. "I had no idea what you were going through. I wish I'd known. I might have been able to help. I've had three of my own and I know what post natal depression is."

"That's nice of you, Mrs Oliver, but I don't think anyone could have helped."

"Mr Carey was nearly out of his mind with worry. I've never seen a man age so much." The woman put the large fish kettle on the electric range. "I'm so glad everything has turned out all right and you're back to stay."

Jillane looked over her shoulder at her. "Oh, but I'm not here to stay. It's just over Christmas."

"Oh, dear, I beg your pardon." Mrs Oliver looked flustered. "I was sure Mr

Carey said he'd found a school for the little . . . I must have got it wrong. My hearing's been funny since I had the 'flu last month." She looked anxious. "You won't say . . . "

Jillane forced a grin. "Of course I won't say anything."

No sound came from the sitting-room. Jillane pushed open the door and saw Ash stretched along the settee fast asleep. Pepper, also asleep, was sprawled across him. Both had their mouths open and both looked vulnerable.

Jillane tiptoed to look down at them and thought for the hundredth time how alike they were. Apart from his smattering of grey their hair was an exact match while both had hollowed cheeks and that firm curve to the chin. Their teeth were white and even with prominent canines. Even their hands were the same, the long slender fingers ending in crescent-shaped cuticles and square nails.

As she stared Ash slowly opened his

eyes. He smiled lazily. "Jillane! How beautiful you look! Every man should have such a vision to wake up to."

She glared at him. "I want to talk to you . . . "

"Oh no." He sighed. "Not another confrontation!"

Pepper stirred and woke.

Jillane gazed at two pairs of warm honey-coloured eyes and gave up for the time being.

She waited till Pepper had been read to and put to bed and chose her words carefully so as not to involve Mrs Oliver.

"This week has flown by," she said as she preceded him down the wide staircase. "I can't believe it's almost time to go home. One more full day then . . . "

"Must you go?" He quickened his step to draw level with her as they reached the hall. "Your home could be here."

She faced him. So it was true. He'd meant all along for them to stay. She panicked. What scheme had he in mind? She was his prisoner. How was she going to escape, rescue Pepper?

He was watching her changing expressions. "What's the matter? What have I said?" He sliced his fingers through his hair in a bewildered fashion. "I merely asked you to stay on here. It's the logical conclusion."

"No!"

"Jillane, be reasonable. All together under one roof is the ideal solution. That way we never need to go to court to argue about custody, or even have to consider sharing Pepper. We can genuinely put on a united front."

She stared at him in horror. "You mean be married again?"

"We are married." His eyes hardened.

"I meant . . . live together as man and wife . . . ?"

His smile was mirthless. "You make it sound like a fate worse than death." He opened the sitting-room door for her to enter. "No, that's not what I meant." His tone was clipped, angry.

"If you live here you will have your own room. I shan't bother you."

As you have not 'bothered me' these past weeks, she thought.

"Think about it, Jillane," he urged. "Don't dismiss it out of hand."

"But my job . . . "

"Ah, I've been thinking about that. You really should be involved with Carey's. We have a small fleet of company helicopters. You might like to consider taking them over. You know, keeping check on them, maintaining them, making sure they're where they should be."

She was interested despite herself. It sounded just the kind of work she would enjoy. But she wasn't going to tell him so. Besides it sounded a bit too much like bribery.

She chewed her lower lip. He had taken her completely by surprise and defused all her arguments. What else was new?

The phone rang in the hall and he strode away to answer it. Five minutes later he poked his head round the door to say he was going out.

"Sheridan's car has broken down just outside Palmly. I'm going to give her a tow. Want to come?"

"Couldn't she have rung the AA?"

"Not worth it. She only lives in the village. Coming?"

"No, thanks." She needed time to sort her feelings out and she couldn't do that when he was around, overpowering her emotions with his magnetism, bombarding her with his charm till she did what he wanted.

She smiled grimly to herself. Is that what it was? Magnetism and charm? No wonder she was in a spin every time she encountered him.

Besides, driving with him on an errand of mercy smacked of togetherness and that was the last thing she wanted to foster between them.

He went off whistling, leaving her in a quandary of indecision. She wished he hadn't asked her to stay and upset all her plans again.

The following day Ash took Pepper to the Robin Hood Experience while Jillane finished the packing and washed her hair.

They arrived back in time for dinner and Pepper was full of the lovely school they had been to see on the way home.

"There was only one teacher there because of the holidays," she said excitedly. "But she was nice. Her name was Mrs Bruce. Daddy says I can go there if I like. They have a tennis court and there were horses and lots of other animals . . . "

"I see." Jillane met Ash's gaze over Pepper's head. "It sounds very nice."

"I hope I can go there," said Pepper, skipping away.

Jillane took a deep breath and rounded on Ash.

"You bastard!"

8

ASH was working away from home the next few days and things settled down into a routine. Now that the holiday was over, Sheridan was much more in evidence. Although her office was in the lodge, she was always popping in and out of his study with notebooks and folders and sometimes speaking to him on the phone. Jillane accepted it was all in the cause of business, but could not completely erase her former distrust.

She phoned Matthew to tell him she had agreed to stay on at *Grasslands* for a trial period of one month.

"Ash wore me down till I agreed. And he had Pepper on his side."

"That's it then." Matthew's tone was melancholy. "I shan't be seeing you again. I'd better start looking for another pilot."

"You *will* be seeing me again," she said fiercely. "Because this arrangement isn't going to work. Please keep my job open for me."

"Very well. But I don't like it."

"You're not the only one."

With Ash away there seemed little for her to do. Pepper had made friends with Sam the gardener's children and was happy playing in their tree-house. And the mansion was run very efficiently by the staff. Jillane didn't wish to interfere. She would not be here long enough to make changes.

She was only staying for the month's trial to show willing — so Ash could not accuse her of throwing his plan out before giving it time to work. As soon as the agreed period was up she would be hightailing it back to Denbridge, her duty done. It would be proven, in court if necessary, that she had given the reconciliation a fair chance and it had failed. Then they could get on with the divorce and work something out concerning Ash's access to Pepper.

She was sitting before the fire in the library, reading a history of Palmly village when she heard the trolley being wheeled in. It would be Mrs Oliver with the afternoon tea. Jillane yawned and rubbed the back of her neck. "Ah, just what I could do with."

However it was Ash.

He brought the trolley to the hearth and stood before the fire warming his hands. "What are you reading?"

She showed him.

"Ah, a fascinating subject."

She leaned forward and poured the tea into the delicate porcelain cups. "Have you read all these books?"

"I've read a lot of them, but not all. There are thousands!" He accepted the cup and saucer from her and remained standing with his back to the flames. "This used to be my bolt-hole when I was a kid, where I would hide while my parents were fighting it out."

She looked up sharply. "Oh Ash, I'm sorry, I didn't know."

"Why should you?" His negligent shrug spoke for itself. "It's not something I boast about."

She waited, her very silence inviting him to confide in her.

He took a gulp of tea. "They married to unite two local families but I believe they were in love — to begin with. They parted when I was eleven. My mother moved back to her parents' home the other side of Chesterfield and I stayed here with my father. I don't know which was worse, the battles or the ceasefire, but I hated the travelling to and fro between them."

He got up and placed his cup on the trolley then walked to the window to stare out over the lawns.

She studied his profile, noted the taut mouth, the nerve beating in his jaw, and was filled with compassion for him.

"I vowed it would never happen to one of mine. Correction, I vowed I wouldn't marry and have a child to be put through all that."

He must have heard her sudden intake of breath for he turned. "I hadn't figured on meeting someone like you."

His gaze met and held hers, radiating unexpected warmth. She grew dizzy from its impact.

He demolished the distance between them. "Jillane, it could work!"

She recoiled instinctively from him. "What could?" she asked, knowing full well he referred to their marriage.

"Us." He relieved her of her cup and placed it on the trolley then took hold of her forearms and pulled her gently from the chair. "Our marriage. We never gave it a fair chance. If we tried again, from the start, living together as man and wife . . . "

She shook her head. "But nothing has changed. You still neglect your family when it suits you. You let Pepper down over the Robin Hood Experience."

"That was different. I can explain if you'll let me."

"Spare me the details. I was better off before we met again. I was making a life for myself. I don't want to go backwards."

"If we both made a concerted effort . . . "

"No . . . " She watched him circumspectly. The heat radiating from his eyes was disarming her and she detected a strange yearning in their glowing depths.

"Jillane!" His mouth was at her throat, his hand cupping one breast. "I want you so much."

She trembled violently. His touch was doing wild things to her equilibrium and she threw her head back as an unexpected tidal wave of bliss hit her.

His lips moved to hers in a kiss of such intense passion she had to grab at his jacket to steady herself. Blood pounded in her temples and her flesh was at once on fire for him. "Oh Ash!"

From the hall came the sound of footsteps, coming nearer. They stood back from each other, breathing erratically, and guiltily faced the door as Sheridan knocked and entered.

"I'm sorry to disturb you, Ash." She looked from one flushed face to the other.

Ash recovered quickly. With a glance at his chronograph he exclaimed, "Four o'clock! You're working late for a Saturday."

"I had to come in to phone California. It's morning there." Another glance at Jillane then back to Ash. "Could I speak to you for a moment?" Her lips trembled and she seemed near to tears.

Jillane stared in surprise.

Ash was by her side in a flash. "What ever's the matter?"

"It's . . . " The tears overflowed.

Jillane felt *de trop* and seized the opportunity to escape. What was Sheridan up to now? she wondered as she crossed the hall.

However, it was of no consequence to her. She wouldn't be here much longer. She didn't think she could bear any more tension between herself and Ash. She had to get away before she lost her sanity.

He didn't know how deeply his suggestion had affected her. To live together as man and wife. Her first reaction had been to conjure up those carefree passionate days in Scotland. Then common sense had told her it could never be like that. You couldn't go back. If she thought they could recapture that idyllic time she was kidding herself.

Thanks to Sheridan she'd had a lucky escape just then. And yet . . . her body was still plagued by the promise contained in Ash's touch and its unfulfillment had left her awash with frustration.

He caught up with her later as she was cleaning Pepper's shoes in the kitchen.

"What did Sheridan want?" She hadn't meant to ask but her curiosity got the better of her.

"It's the seventh anniversary of her husband's death. Suddenly it was all too much for her."

"She's a widow? I had no idea."

"Oh yes. Edward was an invalid and she nursed him through his last illness."

"I see."

He smiled gently. "You have nothing to fear from Sheridan."

"I'm not in the least concerned about Sheridan," she declared haughtily, relieved to see Mrs Oliver come in with a bowl of fruit.

Ash shrugged helplessly and went away.

Later that evening she was sitting on the velvet dressing stool in her bedroom brushing her hair, when in the mirror reflection she saw the door open and Ash enter.

He wore a karate-style robe which swung open to reveal his long muscled legs, his hair was damp and he brought with him the manly fragrance of a recent shower.

She watched him turn the key in the lock.

Huskily he said, "Nothing is going to stop me now. Not Sheridan, nor Pepper, nor Mrs Oliver, nor Uncle Tom Cobley and all."

"I'm tired." Jillane stood up and threw the brush into the clutter of jars on the dressing table. "I want to go to bed."

"I'm not stopping you."

"To sleep."

With one finger he traced the outline of her mouth. "You know you don't mean that."

Time stood still as they contemplated each other.

Slowly, deliberately, he pulled her to him. She was trapped against his hard body as his mouth plundered hers. The invasion of his tongue sent a flight of erotic flutterings winging through her bloodstream.

Another moment and he had eased off her robe and nightdress. He paused, transfixed, his eyes taking their fill of her nakedness. Then his tantalising fingers did the walking over her tender flesh.

She stood there motionless, hardly daring to breath as that familiar yearning splintered through her, that aching desire over which she had no control. She couldn't stop him now, even if she'd wanted to, so she surrendered to the inevitable. She loved him, was almost sick with longing for him. There was no going back. Nothing mattered any more but that he should finish what he had started.

Sweeping her into his arms he headed for the bed where he spread her almost reverently among the sheets.

She watched as he cast aside his robe and her need for him became a tangible ache which threatened to drive her mad if not soon attended to. She raised impatient arms to encircle his neck.

"Ash!"

As if it were the signal he had been waiting for, he gave a grunt of satisfaction and his powerful frame pinned her to the bed. It was like being buried under a landslide. For long piquant moments she lay there, inhaling his masculine scent, conscious of his lean muscles, his physical power, before they plunged into a whirling maelstrom of savage ecstasy. She felt the untamed hunger in him — and matched it — till they were swept away on a roller-coaster of passion.

Her spirits soared, her senses were heightened to fever pitch, then came a primeval explosion like a thousand megawatt sunburst in her nerve centre.

She hadn't suspected he could contain such unbridled hunger but she heard the clock down in the hall strike ten o'clock . . . eleven . . . twelve and still he had not finished with her.

★ ★ ★

The pale light of morning flooded the bed, waking Jillane from the depths of slumber. A glance at her watch told her

215

it was long past breakfast time.

Her body still pulsated to the rhythm of Ash's lovemaking. She lay with her back to him, encircled in his embrace, her body aligned with his, shoulder to shoulder, chest to spine, bent knee to bent knee. She could tell from his steady breathing that he was asleep.

Stealthily so as not to wake him she slewed round to gaze at his ruffled hair and the dark stubble on his jaw. She smiled deliriously, reliving the precious moments they had shared.

Slowly his eyes opened. "Jillane, darling!"

With a quick movement he gathered her closer to him and held her captive while he kissed her.

"You were wonderful!" he whispered.

"So were you."

He laughed. "I could eat the proverbial horse."

"Hm, me too!"

They showered together, laughing and caressing, then each dried the other with the big fluffy towels.

Back in the bedroom he fastened his robe while she padded to the wardrobe to find some clothes to wear. She saw her naked reflection in the full-length mirror and stopped in her tracks. Her skin glowed, her eyes sparkled and the expression on her face conveyed total contentment.

He came to stand behind her. "There." He sounded strangely triumphant. "I don't think we shall have any differences now. Do you, my darling?" He slipped his arms round her waist. "The marriage is consummated. We are one again, darling." He kissed her bare shoulder. "I shall have my things moved in here . . . "

She wriggled free and spun round to face him as an alarming thought struck her. He hadn't . . . couldn't . . . wouldn't . . . make love to her for the sole reason of getting his own way finally regarding Pepper!

Oh yes he would! Suddenly she felt very fragile, as breakable as fine porcelain. One knock and she could shatter into smithereens.

She shrank from him and grabbed up her robe.

"Why, what's the matter?" he asked. "You don't like this room? We can use my room if you prefer but this is bigger . . . "

She blinked rapidly to keep her tears at bay. "Oh, you loathsome creature! You made love to me just to make sure we were properly wed, to make divorce more difficult. So Pepper would have two parents . . . "

He contemplated her steadily. "Is that what you think?" His gaze grew hostile. "I've said it before, you have a poor opinion of me."

"What else am I to think?" she cried. "You are devious . . . You would do anything . . . "

"Thank you very much."

"What a fool I've been! Thinking you could ever change. Oh, why did you have to come back into my life?"

He glared at her. "All right, you've seen through me. I made love to you for the exact reason you said — to keep Pepper!"

She thought she detected a note of irony in his tone but couldn't be sure.

He had not made any declaration of love, she noted.

Because he could not.

"I hate you!" she shouted. "I've always hated you . . . "

As if he hadn't heard he turned and strode from the bedroom.

The tears overflowed at last. She dabbed at them angrily, hating her weakness. Her tears were not important.

The important thing was to get as far away as possible from the man who would callously use love as a weapon.

9

JILLANE opened all the cupboards and piled everything on the bed. In her desperation she had rung Matthew and he was driving to Derbyshire to fetch her.

She had spent the time since then mulling over a wild plan to marry Matthew as soon as she was in a position to do so. Living with him would ensure Ash left her alone.

Pepper had made a fuss when she discovered they were leaving but Jillane told her it was only for a short time.

There would be trouble from Ash over her removal of the child, she was aware, but she couldn't worry about that now. She would have to resort to the courts after all.

As eleven o'clock approached Jillane kept watch from the window, dreading the thought that Ash might return from his office before Matthew arrived. She was already hurting enough. And a nasty scene would be traumatic for Pepper.

At last she saw Matthew's BMW coming in through the gates and she hustled Pepper down to the hall to meet him.

He kissed her cheek and ruffled Pepper's hair. The girl pulled a face at him.

"Is this everything?" he asked, picking up the cases.

Jillane nodded.

He looked guardedly at Pepper. "Where's . . . ?"

"Out. I've left a note with Mrs Oliver."

He put Pepper in the back and fastened her seatbelt. Busy dressing her Cindy doll and singing to herself, she did not appear interested in their conversation.

As Matthew drove out onto the main road Jillane was agitated to see Ash's Lotus approaching. But the BMW had darkened glass in the windows and she knew that, although he probably recognised the vehicle, he couldn't see its occupants.

"Look, there's Daddy," cried Pepper waving.

Jillane relaxed as the danger passed and experienced an odd feeling of anti-climax. She hoped fervently she was doing the right thing. Now that they were definitely on their way she suspected she hadn't given the matter enough thought. She should have learned by now that running away seldom solved anything. In fact it just aggravated the situation and created more problems.

"Matthew . . . "

"Hello!" He glanced in the rear-view mirror. "There's a police car following, with all lights flashing. I'd better pull over to let them pass."

He did so but the police car slewed to a halt in front of them and two officers got out.

They walked slowly towards them

and Jillane's heart sank with a terrible foreboding.

"Excuse me, sir," said the sergeant. "We have reason to believe this car is stolen."

"Stolen?" Matthew looked dumbfounded as he climbed out. "But that's preposterous."

He produced documents to prove he was the owner and the two officers browsed through them in a leisurely manner.

A moment later another car screeched to a halt behind them and Ash alighted.

"Daddy!" cried Pepper, struggling with the door lock.

Matthew had left his door open and Ash reached in to release the catch and his daughter. She leapt into his arms and he carried her to the Lotus.

"Hang on a minute," said Jillane scrambling from the car and running after them. "What do you think you're doing?"

"I'm taking Pepper home."

She opened her mouth to speak and

he warned sharply, "Watch what you say in front of *l'enfant*!"

He had strapped Pepper into the narrow rear seat. "That's always been your answer to everything." He slammed the door shut. "Running away."

"Give me back my child," she hissed as panic seized her. "You'll never be allowed to keep her."

His smile chilled her to the bone. "I wouldn't be too sure of that. Possession is nine-tenths of the law, I believe."

A finger of fear edged along her spine. "Please, Ash, you wouldn't be so cruel . . . "

"Like you, you mean?"

She began pulling frenziedly at the handle, but he had locked the door. "Give me my child!"

He restrained her. "Stop shouting. You don't want to frighten Pepper with your wild antics."

Jillane turned back to the police car. "We'll see what the law has to say."

"Oh, I shouldn't bother." He shrugged loosely. "They're friends of mine."

Her mouth gaped. "You mean . . . ?" She pressed her lips into a censorious line. "Oh, how could you!"

"Yes, Matthew will be quite a time with them, I fear."

"I want Pepper . . . "

Ash walked round the car. "Now you know how it feels. You don't like it, do you?"

"Please . . . "

"Oh, didn't I tell you?" He opened the front passenger door for her. "You're invited as well."

She climbed in, relief pouring over her like a healing spring.

"Silly Mummy," said Ash sliding in beside her and directing his words over his shoulder. "She didn't know I was playing a game."

Now that Pepper hadn't been snatched, Jillane's concern was for Matthew. "Hadn't you better go over and put the record straight for the poor man?"

"No. Serves him right."

"But he's an innocent bystander . . . "

The car engine sprang to life, drowning Ash's laugh. "Innocent bystander, my foot!" He checked the rear view mirror and saw Pepper was absorbed with fixing a tiara to her doll's hair. "If he wants to pick forbidden fruit he should expect the farmer to come after him."

"He might sue for wrongful arrest."

"Good lord! He hasn't been arrested. He's merely helping the police with their enquiries."

"Oh!" She cried, remembering. "My things and Pepper's are in his boot."

"No problem." He reached for his car phone. "I'll ask the police to confiscate them and hold on to them for me."

★ ★ ★

The moment they arrived at *Grasslands* Ash said, "Come along, Pepper. Let's see if Mrs Oliver's got your lunch ready."

To Jillane he said, "I'll be with you in a moment."

They went off hand in hand and

Jillane took herself to the library. She hadn't long to wait.

"What in heaven's name got into you?"

He closed the door and stood with his back against it. "Taking my daughter back to Denbridge without telling me? Hell! You don't change, do you? The first time you ran away from me, in Scotland, I accepted that you were too young to understand, that I should have been more patient with you, but you're older now and I expected you to have matured. How wrong I was! The fact is, you're never going to change."

She paled at this tirade but acknowledged most of it was true. "I'm sorry if I gave you a fright."

"Well, I warn you, if you ever try such a stunt again I shall have Pepper made a ward of court."

He stormed off, leaving the threat hanging in the air.

She paced the library lost in thought. There would be no more attempts at leaving. If she tried again she would lose her child. She was his prisoner as surely as if he had her under lock and key.

She was not looking forward to phoning Matthew but felt she owed him something. He was furious with her and accused her of deliberately using him to make Ash jealous.

Poor Matthew! She *had* used him. But not to make Ash jealous, she was sure. For Ash to be jealous he must love her first and that was so unlikely it would be hilarious were it not so tragic.

★ ★ ★

The first week in January Pepper started her new school. Although it had been arranged that Sam, the gardener, would ferry her to and fro each day, the first time was special. Jillane and Ash set aside their differences to go with her and see her settled in.

Jillane shed a few tears as they drove away and Ash was unusually silent.

She watched his strong profile and her heart gave a little flutter. He hadn't moved his things into her room. He hadn't touched her since their wild night of passion. Subsequent nights had been spent tossing in the misery of her own making, thinking of all she was missing and wishing it hadn't to be like this. She had admitted to herself that she still loved him, in spite of everything, and she didn't think she could bear his indifference much longer.

The following day he went off to Edinburgh for a week to attend a trade fair.

Jillane wandered listlessly around the house wishing she had something to occupy her. She thought of the job he had mentioned about her being in charge of Carey helicopters. She hoped it was still on offer and decided she must tackle him about it when he returned.

After he had been gone three days she went to the kitchen and asked Mrs

Oliver if there was anything she could do for her.

"Why don't you clear out the playroom?" the woman suggested. "That place has been locked up far too long and I'm wasting my time dusting every week. You could make it into a nice den for Pepper."

Jillane's heart seemed to miss a beat. "What playroom?"

Mrs Oliver was in the throes of returning a heavy joint of lamb to the oven after basting it and she was too hot and bothered to notice Jillane didn't know what she was talking about. "Miss Sheridan keeps the key."

Sheridan was tapping away at her computer when Jillane ventured into the lodge office. She looked up and grinned. "Shan't be a moment. I'll just finish this column."

Jillane smiled back. She had accepted that Sheridan was no threat as far as Ash was concerned and thought, given the chance, they could be friends.

She watched the cyclamen-varnished

nails fly over the keys. It was a constant surprise that this glamorous woman, who belonged in modelling, appeared so at home here running Ash's empire and lording it over an army of typists at the Chesterfield head office. Why couldn't people stay in the pigeon-holes she had marked for them?

"What are you doing?"

"A survey of insurance claims against us during the past twelve months." Sheridan tore off the print-out and showed Jillane the entries. "This last concerns the nightwatchman at the Chesterfield plant. You know, the one who was coshed during that break-in over Christmas."

"Oh dear," said Jillane. "I didn't know there'd been a break-in or that anyone was coshed. Is he okay?"

"Bert's coming along nicely. But didn't Ash tell you about it?" Sheridan sounded most surprised. "I know he dashed over there the moment he heard, to see if he could do anything. Bert's wife said he was really kind."

That must have been when he'd had to postpone the Robin Hood Experience, thought Jillane, mortified to recall she had accused him of neglecting Pepper over Christmas when it had been a mission of mercy on his part. What had she said? 'Spare me the details'. It sounded so callous.

"Well, what can I do for you?" asked Sheridan.

Jillane decided to pretend she knew what she was talking about. "I'd like to clear out the playroom. It needs doing."

"Good idea." Sheridan delved into a drawer and searched through a box of assorted keys. She read a label. "Yes, here it is." Another smile broke out as she handed it over. "I'm glad you're doing something about that room. I always thought Ash was morbid keeping it as it was." She looked pensive. "But I could understand his motives. I kept my husband's room exactly as it was for years after he died."

Jillane nodded sympathetically.

She studied the key label. 'Playroom. Annexe.' "Thanks, Sheridan. See you later."

The annexe, built at the turn of the century, was a large single-storied extension at the rear of the mansion. As far as she knew it wasn't used these days, except for storing surplus furniture.

She let herself in to what was a long corridor. Three doors led off from it and she tried them all. The first two were not locked and she gazed in rooms where desks and office chairs had been untidily dumped to gather dust.

The third door was locked. With her heart beating faster than usual she applied the key. It fitted and turned.

The first thing which met her eyes was the splendid carpet, a rich duck-egg blue embellished with cream whorls. Standing on it were brightly-coloured little chairs, and tables containing an assortment of fluffy animals, books, bricks, dolls, puzzles and music boxes.

Around the walls stood larger toys — a rocking horse, a pedal car, a dolls' pram and a Wendy house. The wallpaper and matching curtains bore a treasure island design and various nursery rhyme mobiles hung from the ceiling.

In front of a gas fire with imitation coals and safety guard lay a white mock-fur rug fashioned like a polar bear skin complete with a friendly-looking head.

The place was a child's paradise.

★ ★ ★

Tears suddenly blinded her and she groped for the door. Poor Ash! He had wanted the baby all along and had made this secret playroom in readiness. She had misjudged him and broken his heart when she told him of the stillbirth. She remembered the pearl necklace which lay in her drawer, her present on the delivery of his child. Hope surged in her heart. If she had been wrong about one thing there was a chance she could have been wrong about everything. Even his love for her!

She got the door open and to her great surprise came face to face with Ash.

She dabbed frantically at her eyes with her sleeves. "Wh . . . what are you doing home? I thought . . . "

"Don't cry, Jillane." His warm arms round her brought instant comfort. "Sheridan said you'd asked for the keys to this room."

"Oh Ash! Why didn't you tell me about . . . all this?"

"It was to be a surprise for you and our baby."

His tone confirmed his hurt, an exposed nerve, sending more tears splashing onto her cheeks. "You wanted our child! And I thought you married me to please my father."

He held her close. "When you ran out on me in Scotland I was sick with disappointment. I tried to trace you, but the woman in charge of your party — Miss Wooding, was it? — wouldn't give me your address. I didn't even know which county you lived in. I armed myself with the phone books but it was hopeless. Do you know how many Pritchards there are in the land?"

"I didn't think . . . "

He stroked her oaten curls. "I endeavoured to get on with my life, but you haunted my dreams. When your father turned up and told me you were pregnant I figured that you'd marry me if only to give the child a name. Keith put no pressure on me whatsoever."

"Why did you want to marry me?"

"Because I loved you."

He had spoken in the past tense, she noted. If only she'd known. Things could have been so different. She'd had everything and tossed it all away.

He went on, "I guessed you only married me to please your father but I reckoned once we were wed I'd make you fall in love with me."

"Is that why you kept going away and leaving me?" she couldn't resist asking.

"It couldn't be helped. We were opening a new factory in Senegal and I was needed to sort out the disappearance of some vital machinery. Without it the local people could not work. I discovered it hadn't been sent because the money had been embezzled. Big names were involved. The factory was, *is*, their lifeline. Think of it, the possible destruction of a whole neighbourhood. It needed someone who dared to face despots and demand action — me! The Senegal problems didn't go away, they continued right into our marriage."

"Why didn't you tell me all this before you abandoned me in Scotland?"

"Frankly I didn't think you'd understand and I had no time." He hooked a finger under her chin and forced her to look at him. "And let's face it, you were behaving like a spoilt brat." He kissed the tear-stained cheeks. "Because you

237

were a spoilt brat."

This time she did not argue. In retrospect everything he said was true.

"I should have told you and given you the benefit of the doubt. It was arrogant of me to presume you were too young to understand why the job should come before you and the baby."

"Yes, it was."

"All that's finished now," he said. "I delegate these days."

She glanced round the playroom. "What's going to happen to all this?"

"Well, it was for Pepper but she's too old for most of it now. She might like the Wendy house, and the pram . . . I'll let her choose what she wants. The rest can go to Oxfam." He thought for a moment, his eyes fired with imagination. "We could turn it into a den for her. Later on she could use it for doing her homework in. And when she's a teenager she can have it as a disco! There's a firm in Edinburgh . . . "

"Yes, why aren't you there?" she

asked, reminded. "You said you'd be away a week."

"I couldn't settle. You seemed so unhappy and it was all my fault." His voice grew husky. "Don't leave *Grasslands*. I need you here."

"I'm not leaving. I can't . . . not without Pepper." That wasn't the only reason and she must tell him now. She'd lived with her heart in the clouds far too long. It was time to come down to earth. "Besides, I love you too much to leave."

He gazed at her in wonder. "Jillane, is it true?" He lay his palm against her cheek. "My darling, I should have swallowed my foolish pride and told you ages ago how much you mean to me. I love you, Jillane. I've never stopped loving you." His lips were hard on hers. "All these years you have been constantly on my mind."

She could hardly believe her ears. "Oh Ash!"

He put his hand under her chin. "Forgive me, Jillane, for making you cry. That wasn't my intention. I've been so insensitive to your feelings."

"It's you who should forgive me. I'm the one who's been insensitive."

"We won't argue about who's to blame." He cuddled her close. "It's a waste of time and we've wasted too much already. I feel as if I want to get to know you all over again." His eyes shone suddenly. "Let's take a honeymoon! I have a Greek island . . . "

"I know. Could we take Pepper?"

"Of course. It'll mean waiting till the Easter break."

"What about her passport? Her name . . . She thinks of herself as Pepper Talbot."

"We'll change it to Carey by deed poll. We'll tell her they made a mistake on her birth certificate." He squinted down at her. "Well, they did, didn't they?"

Jillane averted her eyes. "Sorry."

He smiled tenderly. "It's all right, darling. It doesn't matter any more."

They smiled crazily at each other.

Jillane linked her arm through his. "Sam will have fetched her from school. She'll be having her tea. Let's go and tell her about the holiday!"

"Okay." He pulled her gently back into the room and closed the door. Staring mischievously at the polar bear rug, he murmured, "That looks nice and soft."

Puzzled, she followed his gaze. "I don't understand. I thought we were going to tell Pepper . . . "

"We are." He kicked the switch on the fire to 'on'. "But not just yet."

THE END

Other titles in the
Linford Romance Library:

A YOUNG MAN'S FANCY
Nancy Bell

Six people get together for reasons of their own, and the result is one of misunderstanding, suspicion and mounting tension.

THE WISDOM OF LOVE
Janey Blair

Barbie meets Louis and receives flattering proposals, but her reawakened affection for Jonah develops into an overwhelming passion.

MIRAGE IN THE MOONLIGHT
Mandy Brown

En route to an island to be secretary to a multi-millionaire, Heather's stubborn loyalty to her former flatmate plunges her into a grim hazard.

WITH SOMEBODY ELSE
Theresa Charles

Rosamond sets off for Cornwall with Hugo to meet his family, blissfully unaware of the shocks in store for her.

A SUMMER FOR STRANGERS
Claire Hamilton

Because she had lost her job, her flat and she had no money, Tabitha agreed to pose as Adam's future wife although she believed the scheme to be deceitful and cruel.

VILLA OF SINGING WATER
Angela Petron

The disquieting incidents that occurred at the Vatican and the Colosseum did not trouble Jan at first, but then they became increasingly unpleasant and alarming.

DOCTOR NAPIER'S NURSE
Pauline Ash

When cousins Midge and Derry are entered as probationer nurses on the same day but at different hospitals they agree to exchange identities.

A GIRL LIKE JULIE
Louise Ellis

Caroline absolutely adored Hugh Barrington, but then Julie Crane came into their lives. Julie was the kind of girl who attracts men without even trying.

COUNTRY DOCTOR
Paula Lindsay

When Evan Richmond bought a practice in a remote country village he did not realise that a casual encounter would lead to the loss of his heart.

ENCORE
Helga Moray

Craig and Janet realise that their true happiness lies with each other, but it is only under traumatic circumstances that they can be reunited.

NICOLETTE
Ivy Preston

When Grant Alston came back into her life, Nicolette was faced with a dilemma. Should she follow the path of duty or the path of love?

THE GOLDEN PUMA
Margaret Way

Catherine's time was spent looking after her father's Queensland farm. But what life was there without David, who wasn't interested in her?

HOSPITAL BY THE LAKE
Anne Durham

Nurse Marguerite Ingleby was always ready to become personally involved with her patients, to the despair of Brian Field, the Senior Surgical Registrar, who loved her.

VALLEY OF CONFLICT
David Farrell

Isolated in a hostel in the French Alps, Ann Russell sees her fiancé being seduced by a young girl. Then comes the avalanche that imperils their lives.

NURSE'S CHOICE
Peggy Gaddis

A proposal of marriage from the incredibly handsome and wealthy Reagan was enough to upset any girl — and Brooke Martin was no exception.

A DANGEROUS MAN
Anne Goring

Photographer Polly Burton was on safari in Mombasa when she met enigmatic Leon Hammond. But unpredictability was the name of the game where Leon was concerned.

PRECIOUS INHERITANCE
Joan Moules

Karen's new life working for an authoress took her from Sussex to a foreign airstrip and a kidnapping; to a real life adventure as gripping as any in the books she typed.

VISION OF LOVE
Grace Richmond

When Kathy takes over the rundown country kennels she finds Alec Stinton, a local vet, very helpful. But their friendship arouses bitter jealousy and a tragedy seems inevitable.

CRUSADING NURSE

I   ho
o   n's
e   a

l   ful
e   gle
a

d a
me
out
nt.

n's
cer,
it
ing